Patrick's Charm

Book 2, The Bride Train

E.E. BURKE

Patrick's Charm is a work of fiction.
Names, characters, places and incidents are the product of the
author's imagination or are used fictitiously.

Cover Design by Erin Dameron-Hill
Train photography by Matthew Malkeiwicz
Digital formatting by Author E.M.S.

Published by E.E. Burke
ISBN-13: 978-0-9969822-7-6

Author's Note

The Bride Train is inspired by a series of true events that took place in southeastern Kansas shortly after the Civil War. After the government opened up former Indian land, one of the railroads finagled a deal to purchase the entire tract. Settlers who had moved onto the land and filed claims under "preemption" were forced to broker deals with the new owner.

By 1869, riots broke out in protest of railroad land policies. Angry settlers burned ties and tore up track as fast as the railroad could put it down. Things got so bad that President Grant sent troops into Kansas to quell the violence. A more peaceful solution was proposed: a program sponsoring the immigration of single young ladies into Kansas to become brides and provide a "calming influence" on the unruly men. I couldn't find any evidence this program got off the ground. But what a great romance series idea!

The Bride Train is first mentioned in my debut romance novel, Her Bodyguard, which is set against the same series of events in a different location. This scene inspired me to conceive an entire series about a railroad matchmaking service.

Patrick's Charm is Book 2 in The Bride Train series. The hero, Patrick O'Shea, is a disabled veteran who desperately needs a lucky break. Research led me to the plight of Irish immigrants who fought in the American Civil War. Many were recruited "fresh off the boat." They had no idea what they were getting into until they were in the thick of battle.

Few men who fought in the Irish Brigade made it home, even fewer returned unscathed. Wounded soldiers were routinely dosed with opium for pain, and many of them became dependent on the painkiller. Opium addiction among former troops was so bad it was given the name, *Soldier's Disease*. Today, it's difficult to imagine the strength it would've taken to cope with injury, addiction and the rigors of starting a new life on the frontier.

Patrick meets his match in Charm LaBelle, who shows up at his saloon looking for a job. Charm's character is loosely based on the famous 19th century actress Lotta Crabtree, who got her start as a child, entertaining miners in San Francisco.

In her impromptu audition, Charm sings two songs that were popular during the war and afterwards. *The Irish Volunteer* you might classify as a fight song for the Irish Brigade. *Lorena* is a ballad sure to bring tears to the eyes of lonely soldiers. If you'd like to hear them, check out versions on YouTube.

– *E.E. Burke*

Dedication

This one is for America's wounded warriors.

Prologue

Taken from an advertisement posted by the Missouri, Fort Scott & Gulf Railroad in Eastern U.S. newspapers:

EVE, FIND YOUR ADAM
IN THE GARDEN OF THE WORLD!

Single young ladies of good reputation desiring to emigrate west for the purpose of marriage may apply to the Young Ladies Immigration Society for free travel to southeastern Kansas, where hardworking settlers are eager to make their acquaintance and become steadfast husbands. Applicants must be free to wed, of marriageable age, preferably between the ages of 18 and 25, without deformities, debts or other encumbrances. Dance hall girls, circus performers and soiled doves need not apply. Must provide references.

From a letter dated April 8, 1870, written by Mrs. A. Langford, president of the Young Ladies Immigration Society and honorable member of the Missouri River, Fort Scott & Gulf Railroad Board of Directors, to Mr. R. Hardt, newly hired land agent in Cherokee County, in regard to the success of the society's matrimonial efforts:

The first bride train arrived in Girard, Kansas, on March 15. These young women, all of them respectable ladies, remained single for no more than a week. They have already had a calming influence on the unrest in Crawford County. We anticipate the same effect will be felt in Cherokee County subsequent to the delivery of more young women who are able to meet the men's matrimonial needs.

However, you must be aware the arrival of the prospective brides did not stop the Land League from stirring up trouble. The insufferable rebels are worse than an infestation of rattlesnakes and used our rally as a distraction. Whilst some men bid for picnic baskets, others slithered off to burn railroad ties. Our loss was catastrophic. Beware, lest the same thing happen to you. The sooner matches are arranged the better.

Rest assured, the railroad's board remains committed to this program, which will have its intended effect. Facilitating marriage isn't solely a benefit to the railroad. It is for the good of the country. Lawlessness and savagery will not have the last word! The West will be settled, one bride at a time.

Chapter One

May 23, 1870,
Centralia Settlement, Cherokee County, Kansas

Lady Luck hadn't been kind to Patrick O'Shea. In fact, she owed him for all the misery she had dealt him. Yet with every year that passed, her debt increased. One day, Luck would turn and smile on him, and pay up. He just had to hold on until then.

Today, like other days, Patrick refused to dwell on his ill luck. Instead, he celebrated someone else's good fortune. His friend, a former English lord, had recently gotten married, and to an Irish lass, no less, one of the twelve women shipped in by the railroad to become brides for local settlers. The couple had come into town to pick up supplies. While his wife visited friends, the husband did what most husbands would do under similar circumstances. He headed for a pub.

Patrick reached to the top shelf and took down a bottle. "A special occasion calls for the best Irish whiskey." He poured two shots and slid one across the bar.

Constantine Valentine had arrived in Centralia a little over a month ago, dressed like a riverboat gambler and showing no interest in putting down roots on an unsettled stretch of land. He surprised everyone when, instead of selling the deed he won in a poker game, he started drilling holes in the ground, looking for coal. He found his black gold and planned to open a mine. Fickle luck favored the Englishman. Patrick wouldn't hold it against him.

Valentine lifted his glass high. He towered over other men, in height as well as upbringing, yet he didn't look down on them like most of his ilk. Another reason to like him. "Here's to your health, O'Shea."

"My health?" Patrick shifted his stance to relieve the constant ache in his hip and back, another trick of Fate, woven into the fabric of his cursed life. A tonic prescribed by the doctor made the pain bearable, but he would never regain the robust health he enjoyed before the war. He dragged his mind away from dismal reality to happier thoughts. "That's not why I poured me best whiskey. We'll drink to your new bride. She's a keeper. If you hadn't gotten 'round to marrying your Irish Rose, I'd be tempted to take her off your hands."

The Englishman cocked an eyebrow, for him an exaggerated gesture. "I'd advise you resist the temptation if you intend to remain in good health, Mr. O'Shea."

Patrick chuckled. "Yeah, I heard you broke Hardt's nose for being too familiar."

"Not one of my prouder moments..." Valentine frowned as he gazed into his glass. "A misunderstanding."

"Funny, Hardt said the same."

Whatever the *misunderstanding*, it had taken the stuffy railroad agent down a peg or two. He was none the worse for it.

Valentine tossed back his drink. "Ah, that is the good stuff. I've noticed the barkeeps out here fill imported whiskey bottles with doctored up homebrew."

Because men wanted cheap liquor, and imported wasn't cheap.

"I only serve that to customers. Not friends."

"Glad I'm considered among the latter." Valentine set his glass on the bar and leaned forward in a manner that suggested he was about to impart a great secret. "A word of advice, my friend. If you're in need of a wife, make the acquaintance of a barber. I have it on very good authority that women prefer smoothly shaven faces."

Patrick stroked the thick beard he'd planned to shave, now that the weather was warming up. Maybe he ought to keep his whiskers if it would save him from the matrimonial disease afflicting other men in the area. "Don't need a wife. I'm looking to hire dancing girls. Gents'll turn out their pockets to watch gals kick up their heels. And I'll pack the house if I get one that can sing pretty songs."

"Seems unlikely you'll find dance hall girls among the ladies who arrived. They've been promised marriage, and I daresay all twelve will be wed within a fortnight, based on how eagerly they're being courted. There aren't enough to go around."

Patrick wiped out the empty glass. His generosity didn't extend to two free drinks. "Decent women, you mean…" The town had its share of whores. But the few who might be considered pretty didn't have a pleasant voice.

Loud curses erupted at one of the tables. Valentine glanced over, and his brow furrowed in a thoughtful frown. "Are you certain you want to add women to the mix?"

Patrick reached behind the bar for the rifle he kept handy. Arguments happened when whiskey was involved. Fights weren't uncommon, either, but he couldn't afford to have what little he owned destroyed. He nodded to a sign over the door. *No fighting. No cheating. No spitting on the floor.*

"I'll add, *keep your hands off the women*, to the house rules."

"You'll have to enforce them."

Patrick held up the rifle.

The Englishman's expression remained doubtful. "You might consider hiring extra help."

Patrick didn't take the remark to be an insult to his manliness. He'd been built like a bull since the age of twelve and could handle himself in a fight despite his injuries. "I'll worry about that when the time comes. First, I got to find the women."

The angry voices faded into grumbles as the quarrelers settled down to their game of cards. Relieved, Patrick returned the gun to its place behind the bar. For the most part, his clientele were peaceful men: farmers and railroad workers, former Union soldiers like him, who came west for cheap land and the promise of riches. They worked at hard, often punishing, labor, and drank to socialize and alleviate their weariness and the frustration that came from dreams bumping up against hard realities. Some visited whores when they needed to slake a different kind of thirst.

Patrick didn't aspire to run a brothel, not even a fancy one. He'd seen too many destitute young women lured into that degraded lifestyle, young women who reminded him of his sisters. He aimed to have the kind of establishment that offered a higher class of entertainment. Nothing too fancy, just a concert saloon that would make him enough money to live comfortably, so he wouldn't have to scratch in the dirt like his father and his grandfather. His goals weren't nearly as grand as when he first set foot in America. At the moment, however, his financial security seemed as far away as the green shores of Ireland.

"Thank you for the drink." Valentine put a silver dollar on the bar.

Patrick pushed the shiny coin back to its owner, offended that his friend thought he'd be charged for the offered drink, or worse, overcharged. Might be the way they did things in England, but not here. "That one's on me."

Valentine regarded him with a puzzled frown. "You wouldn't accept my thanks the other day when you vouched for me to Mr. Hardt. Now you won't accept my money. What will you accept?"

Patrick stuck out his hand. "Your friendship."

He received a firm handshake.

"You already have that." Valentine collected his hat from where he'd set it on the bar. "I'd stay and visit, but I promised Rose I'd take her shopping."

"Domesticated already? That didn't take long."

The Englishman secured his hat with a droll smile. "You should try it O'Shea. It's not a bad state, matrimony."

"I'll have to take your word for it." Patrick kept a smile pasted on to avoid sounding bitter. Having tried and failed at marriage, he was in no hurry to repeat the mistake.

After Valentine left, Patrick retrieved a cleaning cloth and wiped up a spill on the polished surface of the bar. With its ornate carvings and brass footrests, the fancy bar looked out of place on a floor covered in sawdust. Brought in by train all the way from New York, the hand-carved masterpiece had cost him two month's rent. It was worth every hard-earned dollar. The fine piece of furniture made his dreams more substantial, less like wisps of smoke.

Patrick finished off the short pour he allowed himself, savoring the smoky burn of true Irish whiskey. One day, he'd invest in some oak barrels imported from Ireland and start making his own brand—another unrealized dream.

A shadow in the doorway caught his attention. The small figure outlined in the bright light from outside looked female…short, slight, too shapely for a girl. She sallied into the saloon with surprising boldness. Golden curls framed a face with youthful contours, but she possessed the poise of a mature woman. Patrick tried to guess her age, and couldn't. Her yellow silk skirt bunched up in the back in what he assumed was a new style. Gold braid trimmed her black velvet jacket. No farmers' wives he knew wore that get-up.

He didn't wait for her to find whomever she sought, but went straight over to warn her she'd better wait outside. As he approached, she regarded him quizzically. Thick eyelashes a shade darker than her hair framed luminous brown eyes. He hadn't seen many brown-eyed blondes, and it added to the mystery.

"I would like to speak with the owner," she said in a pleasant tone, without a hint of embarrassment, even though her mere presence here could ruin her reputation.

Her delicacy and youthful beauty and something else, perhaps the innocence shining in her eyes, drew out a strong protective urge along with unexpected stirrings of desire.

Patrick didn't take the time to analyze the disturbing reaction. She had to leave. Now. "Miss, you can't be in here."

The young lady gave him the kind of smile a schoolteacher might bestow on a slow child. "The owner, Mr. O'Shea… Do you know where I might find him?"

For some reason, it irritated him that she hadn't figured it out. "I'm Patrick O'Shea."

The mystery woman's smile vanished and she blinked. The news surprised her. Apparently, she expected someone more… Wealthy? Handsome? Accommodating?

In an instant, she recovered her poise and offered him her hand. "Yes, Mr. O'Shea, very nice to meet you."

He grasped her fingers. The rush of heat signaling arousal surprised him so much he dropped her hand like he'd taken hold of a hot coal.

"I saw your advertisement on the side of the building," she said in a blithe tone that indicated she hadn't yet noticed how red his face was getting.

Considering the effect she had on him, he had to get rid of her. Just as soon as he worked out what she wanted. "My advertisement?"

Her lips twisted in a wry smile. "I supposed it was yours. Someone wrote, "Female entertainers wanted.""

"Oh, that...yeah, that's mine. I wrote it..." He caught himself before he kept blabbing on like a fool. Maybe the medicine he took earlier combined with the whiskey had fogged his brain.

"Good." She brightened up after he claimed responsibility. "Then I'm talking to the right person."

"The right person?" He still didn't know why she was here, although now he recognized her as one of the women who had arrived on the bride train earlier in the month. That didn't explain why she would come to the saloon to talk to him about a sign he put up—unless she had an objection. That had to be it. She was one of those busybodies who liked to tell folks what they could and couldn't do.

He crossed his arms over his chest and frowned down at her. "Are you here to tell me I shouldn't be hiring women?"

Confusion flashed across her face, replaced by a look of amusement. "No, Mr. O'Shea...I'm here to apply for the job."

Charm waited for the Irishman who owned the bar to speak again. His speechless reaction didn't surprise her. Employers didn't look at her and think *female entertainer*. More like, *underage innocent*.

Mr. O'Shea didn't look his part, either. Rather than wearing nice woolen trousers and a colorful vest, beneath the bartender's apron he had on denim and duck cloth. No neatly groomed mustache, either. His face sprouted an unkempt beard. He resembled his rough-looking clientele.

She cast a wary look around, beginning to question her spontaneous decision to inquire about the job. Like most saloons out west, the walls were adorned with the heads and horns of dead animals and amateur paintings of scantily clad women. The air smelled of stale beer, cigar smoke and a musky odor she associated with men who bathed infrequently.

The owner, at least, appeared to be clean.

She'd worked in worse places, and this job at least fit her skills, and it was better than an unwanted marriage, which would be her fate if she didn't find some other way to support herself. Disregarding her misgivings, she met Mr. O'Shea's bewildered gaze, and was struck by the unusual color of his eyes, an intriguing blend of blue and green. His best feature, perhaps. Though it was hard to tell with a beard covering half his face.

He still hadn't spoken, which might mean he'd already hired someone and wasn't sure how to tell her. She sincerely hoped that wasn't the case. "Is the position still available?"

Some emotion flickered in his eyes, which might've been interpreted as panic, except that didn't make sense. "No."

"No, it's not available?"

"No, you're not right for the job."

His blunt rejection caught her off guard. Now what?

Signing on as a bride had seemed a clever ruse, until she'd realized she was stuck in an uncivilized settlement with no other means of support. She had run from one danger straight into another. Would she be forced to go from saloon to saloon, begging for work, or worse, accept a stranger's proposal?

The implications of her tenuous situation triggered an avalanche of emotion, and her eyes began to burn. Horrified, she blinked furiously. Real tears? She hadn't cried real tears for ages, much less in front of a stranger who knew nothing—and didn't care—about her predicament.

Alarm registered on his face. He raised his hands, the universal gesture of helplessness men used when confronted with a weeping woman. "Oh no...no miss, don't cry. I didn't mean to give offense, truly. This...this isn't the sort of job you think it is."

His meaning became clear. Heat flooded her face. Angered at being duped, she lost her patience. "Are you saying your sign is a thinly veiled notice for prostitutes? If so, I will insist you change it so as not to lure another innocent woman into your—"

"No!" Above the beard, his cheekbones reddened. He cast a worried look over his shoulder. The customers had turned away from their cards and conversations to watch them, some with curiosity, others with amusement.

Charm enjoyed being on stage but not being gawked at when she wasn't performing. Ignoring the stares, she held the embarrassed owner's gaze, her anger fading. As she had first suspected, she didn't fit the image of what he thought a female entertainer should look like and that accounted for his remark about her not being right for the job. What a relief to hear he wasn't running a brothel. "What type of entertainer are you looking for?"

"O'Shea! What's a man gotta do to get a drink

around here?" The shout came from a man in dusty denims standing at the bar. Rather, weaving. He didn't need another drink.

The owner turned with an imploring look. "See here, Miss. This isn't a place for the likes of nice young ladies like you. I'm sure you'll find yourself a husband without having to entertain anybody…and I need to get back to my customers, so…" He took a step backwards and made a shooing motion with his hands before he turned and strode away, leaving her standing there, slack-jawed.

The finest theaters from San Francisco to St. Louis had clamored for her to appear, and this uncouth Irishman running a shabby saloon out in the middle of nowhere had just shooed her away like he would a stray cat.

Seething, she followed him and spoke to his back as he reached for a bottle on one of the lower shelves behind the bar. "You did not answer my question, sir."

He spun at her remark. That she'd startled him was evidenced by the way he fumbled the bottle, just catching it before it dropped. He set it on the counter with a thud.

The impatient customer stared at her without recognition.

O'Shea didn't recognize her, either, which was a good thing. She'd changed her name, and it seemed unlikely the men out here on the edge of nowhere would've seen her perform.

"What sort of entertainer do you require?" she repeated.

The owner propped his hands on his hips, frowning. "I need dancers. Singers. *Saloon girls*." He emphasized the last to make sure she understood.

She didn't appreciate being treated like she was dimwitted. "I can sing and dance, and I play the banjo. I'm also a good actress and can put on skits. If you hire me, I assure you, your customers will be entertained…and you won't need any *saloon girls*."

Charm hesitated, looking around. There were no other servers. She'd better clarify. "Unless you need to hire women to serve drinks. I don't do that."

The sandy-haired farmer slammed his hat on the surface on the bar and dust went flying. "I say, hire the gal."

O'Shea poured a drink and held out his hand. The customer slapped a coin into his palm. "Thank you, Mr. McLaughlin, for your informed opinion."

"Glad to be of service—" The bleary-eyed patron let out a loud burp. He grinned at her. "S'cuse me miss. I should introduce myself. Bill McLaughlin, head organizer for the Land League."

O'Shea put his hand on the bar in between her and McLaughlin. The gesture appeared strangely protective. "If you would give us a moment…"

"Oh, sure…" Mr. McLaughlin touched his fingers to his forehead in a drunken salute and staggered back to a table where the other men clapped him on the back. Perhaps he'd been put up to the interruption.

The owner turned to her with a frown. "Look, miss…"

"Labelle." He hadn't bothered to ask.

"Miss Labelle. I'm sure you sing pretty, but what I'm looking for is…" He droned on with a tedious repetition. There would be no convincing him by listing her qualifications. A try-out would be easier if his establishment had a stage, but she could manage without.

She hoisted herself up on the bar. Fortunately, her acrobatic training had made her strong and agile.

"What are you doing?" He swiped at her skirts. She hopped out of his way, to the end of the bar. Fortunately, he wasn't quick. In fact, he appeared to have a limp. That wouldn't stop him from dragging her off the bar if she didn't do something to impress him.

Facing the crowd, she broke out in a rousing song she suspected Mr. O'Shea had heard before, if he hadn't sung it himself.

> *"My name is Tim McDonald,*
> *I'm a native of the Isle,*
> *I was born among old Erin's bogs*
> *when I was but a child.*
> *My father fought in 'Ninety-eight for liberty so dear;*
> *He fell upon old Vinegar Hill, like an Irish volunteer.*
> *Then raise the harp of Erin, boys,*
> *the flag we all revere—*
> *We'll fight and fall beneath its folds,*
> *like Irish volunteers!"*

The customers, after staring at her for a moment, began to clap along. A few men leapt up and joined in, singing. One man even climbed on a table. He held out his arms to her, as if he wanted a hug.

A thrill shot through her and her spirits soared, the feeling she always experienced when bathed in the adulation of a crowd. Warming to the role, she bent down, took an empty glass from a surprised customer and held it high, doing a jig while she sang.

> *"When I was driven from my home*
> *by an oppressor's hand,*
> *I cut my sticks and greased my brogues,*
> *and came o'er to this land.*
> *I found a home and many friends,*
> *and some that I love dear.*
> *Be jabbers! I'll stick to them like bricks*
> *and an Irish volunteer.*

Then fill your glasses up, me boys,
and drink a hearty cheer,
To the land of our adoption
and the Irish volunteer!"

The men cheered and stomped as she sang. The man on the table began to do the jig along with her. When she finished, she took a flourishing bow, and then hopped off the bar—right into Mr. O'Shea's arms.

Her heart, already pounding, sped up. She stared at him, more surprised by her shivering response than by his quick reflexes. This hadn't been part of the plan. She wouldn't willingly jump into any man's arms, much less a stranger's.

The men cheered louder. Coins plinked on the bar as they threw money and yelled for another song.

Her skin grew warm and the thrill heightened, a physical response due to the crowd's enthusiastic response, of course. Not the result of being cradled in the arms of a surly Irish saloonkeeper with eyes that reminded her of the sea on a sunny day.

What was she thinking? She didn't care about the color of his eyes. The impromptu ending had worked out perfectly. She would continue the act to its conclusion. Looping her arms around his neck, she put on a big smile. "I think that qualifies as entertainment, don't you?"

Chapter Two

*P*atrick breathed heavily, and it wasn't due to exertion. The little singer in his arms weighed less than a cask of cider, and sure didn't feel like one. He'd feared she might hurt herself when she jumped off the bar, but even that didn't account for the pounding excitement in his chest.

The song, that's what caused this reaction. *The Irish Volunteer* was the last song he and his brother sang together, while marching through the mud on the way to Fredericksburg. Hearing it again in a strong, beautiful voice had shaken him to the core.

"When do I start?" Miss LaBelle asked breathlessly.

Patrick looked into her flushed, smiling face, and the words needed to send her on her way stuck in his throat. When she had finished singing and then leapt as if she expected him to catch her, he'd reacted instinctively. She might've planned for this, thinking to manipulate him into doing her bidding. That was something Kathleen would've done.

By the auld sod! He wouldn't be twisted around another woman's little finger.

He dropped his right arm and Miss Labelle's feet hit the floor. He kept his left arm around her until he was certain she had her balance. Then he stepped back.

A coin struck the side of his head and bounced off. He sought the culprit with a scowl.

Every man was on his feet.

"Let her sing, dummkopf!" a Dutchman shouted.

"Hire the girl, you fool!" McLaughlin heaved another coin. Patrick raised his hand and caught this one.

"Sing for us, darlin'!" a drunken railroad worker howled.

They loved her. They loved her so much they were throwing money. Patrick came to his senses. He'd be a fool to send her away. The odds of finding another woman who could sing and dance like this one were nil. This was the break in the clouds he'd been waiting for, even if he couldn't quite believe his…

No, he wouldn't call it *luck*. That would jinx him for sure.

He leaned over and whispered. "You can start right now."

Her lips curved into a pleased smile.

"What's your given name, Miss LaBelle?"

"Charm."

His breath caught somewhere just above his pounding heart. It was a sign so obvious even he couldn't miss it. Finally, the day had come. Luck was smiling on him.

If he hired this girl and customers kept throwing money, he could soon afford to fix up the place. O'Shea's would become known as the best spot in the Neutral Lands for entertainment. He would be rich and successful, like he'd dreamed when he first stepped off the boat in America, before he got lured into fighting a war that wasn't his and his life had gone to hell. Some higher power—God, Fate, Luck, maybe they were all one and the same—had decided he'd suffered enough and had granted him a charm.

He reached over, grasped her hand and held it up. Turning to the crowd, he shouted. "Meet Miss Charm LaBelle, O'Shea's new entertainer!"

Enthusiastic cheers went up.

She glanced over with approval shining in her eyes, and his heart melted like warm butter.

Alarmed at her affect on him, he let go of her hand.

Charm sashayed around to the front of the bar and began to croon a familiar ballad that Patrick had heard around crackling campfires in the loneliest hours of the night. More than five years had passed since those hellish times, but hearing *Lorena* brought it all back in a rush.

By the time she started the second verse, there wasn't a dry eye in the place.

"A hundred months have passed, Lorena,
Since last I held that hand in mine,
And felt the pulse beat fast, Lorena,
Though mine beat faster far than thine.
A hundred months, 'twas flowery May,
When up the hilly slope we climbed,
To watch the dying of the day,
And hear the distant church bells chime.
We loved each other then, Lorena,
Far more than we ever dared to tell..."

As she sang, she wove her way through the saloon, passing by each table, lightly touching men's shoulders, acknowledging them with a sympathetic nod. Kindness and empathy flowed out of her in a cool, pure stream.

The men gazed upon her, enthralled, and none more so than Patrick. The yearning ache in his chest intensified, his vision blurred. What an unexpected treasure. An angel, come to life...and to think she had leapt into *his* arms. Every man in the room had fallen in love with her, but she belonged to him. His Charm.

Patrick shook his head to clear the absurd daydream. *His?* She was no more his than the bright blue sky or the warm sunshine or the sweet smells of spring. Whether or not she'd been sent to help him, he couldn't be so brainless as to let his emotions drag him into another heartbreak; and Charm was heartbreak personified. She hadn't shown any man, including him, particular interest, yet she'd woven a spell that made them all believe they were special.

He turned his back on her and the haunting strains of the song, fighting to regain his composure. Working with her, seeing her daily, held more danger than a forest filled with wily Rebs. She wouldn't kill him. But if he let himself fall for her, she'd make him wish he were dead.

After she finished singing, she returned behind the bar. She held out her skirt to carry more coins the men had given her. "I'd suggest putting a jar on the counter...unless you want to keep catching the money they throw."

Her cheeky remark amused him. She was good and she knew it. Her rightful pride in a job well done made her all the more appealing.

Patrick resisted the urge to pull her into his arms and kiss her soundly. Instead, he fished an empty jar from behind the bar. In the meantime, Charm stacked the coins. Her take for two songs included several silver dollars. He did a quick calculation of what they could make in a week, and his mouth went dry. When Lady Luck decided to pay up, she did so in abundance.

"I'll take half," she announced.

"This time." He corrected her to let her know she wouldn't be driving the bargain. "We still need to discuss the financial arrangements."

Her brow furrowed. What he said displeased her. Even if she ended up with half, he couldn't let her have it without serious negotiation, or he'd be seen as namby-pamby.

"All right. We'll talk tomorrow."

"You're leaving?" He hoped to have her perform tonight.

She scraped coins into a small purse attached by a decorative chain to a belt around her tiny waist. "I didn't come prepared to start right away."

Already negotiating. Better not seem too eager and lose any advantage he might have. "That's fine. You can come and go as you please, so long as you aren't late for your performances."

She didn't break eye contact, which for some reason thrilled him. He could lose himself in those big brown eyes.

"You ain't leavin' us now, are you Charm?" McLaughlin's mournful query broke the trance.

Patrick blinked, at the same time Charm jerked her attention to the men leaning on the bar, gazing at her like hopeful puppies. She'd won their utter devotion with two sentimental songs. A fact that was both humorous and sobering.

She eyed her adoring fans warily. McLaughlin puckered up and blew her a kiss. Something akin to fear flickered across her face before she shuttered it behind a polite smile. Odd, how she could dance and sing and parade around in front of these men, but when they got up close, she grew skittish.

"Roll in your tongues, boys..." Patrick took a moment to refill the men's drinks. She needn't worry. He wouldn't let anyone near enough to hurt her. "Miss LaBelle will be back. I'll post a schedule so everybody can see when she's performing."

As she turned to leave, he caught her arm. Didn't

want her getting away without confirming when she'd return. "Be back early, so we can talk before I open up."

She stared at his grip with surprise, and then pulled away, hugging the spot where his hand had been. He hadn't grabbed her tight enough to hurt her. Perhaps she found his touch offensive. Odd that she would decide that now.

"How early?" she asked.

"Eight."

"I'll be here by ten. That should give us sufficient time to discuss a fair arrangement." She hesitated. "We should probably draw up an agreement."

In other words, a handshake wasn't sufficient.

"You mean, write it down? We don't need that. If I make a deal, I'll honor it."

The hesitation, there it was again. "Yes, I'm sure your word is good. But, I don't know you well enough to trust what you will or won't do."

She'd trusted him enough to leap into his arms. It was on the tip of his tongue to say so, except he wasn't so unwise as to insult her like she had insulted him. At least knowing she didn't welcome his attentions would make it easier to keep his hands to himself.

"Fine, then. I don't know you, either. So we'll put everything in writing.

She took a step backwards. Her uncertainty or dislike or fear, or whatever it was, annoyed him. He'd done nothing more than offer her a job.

"Until tomorrow, then."

"No later than ten," he reminded her. "Maybe we ought to put that in writing, too."

"I'll be here." Wounded reproach flashed across her fact an instant before she turned with a swirl of skirts and left.

He considered going after her to apologize for his unkind remark. Better not to get off on the wrong foot.

Then again, he couldn't allow her to lead him in a merry dance, or he would lose what little advantage he had. She would be back because she wanted the job. They would come to some agreeable compromise, and then he would sign her blasted agreement. It would serve as a constant reminder of the danger of becoming too attached to a good luck charm.

Charm left the saloon more flustered and uncertain than when she had arrived. She'd blamed the thrill she'd experienced on the excitement brought about by the crowd's enthusiastic response. When the Irishman touched her arm, the same thing happened again. She couldn't blame that on the crowd.

Her unexpected attraction to the saloon owner confused and frightened her. Having managed to escape the proverbial frying pan, jumping into the fire with Mr. O'Shea would be foolish indeed. For one, she didn't know him. He might expect favors as part of their deal. Or was she reading him wrong? She hated it, this uncertainty. All her life she had worked in places where men gathered and hadn't feared them. Not before Simon had given her a reason to be afraid.

She should heed her misgivings and not return. What did it matter if she didn't show up? Mr. O'Shea would just think she had changed her mind.

Crossing the street was fraught with the usual dangers—ruts deep enough to swallow her to her kneecaps in slick mud, interspersed with piles of pungent manure. She hurried past a flat bed loaded with building materials, and ignored the catcalls and whistles from men who wanted to get her attention. The town and surrounding area had upwards of four hundred inhabitants, most of them male, and most of those the coarse variety, the sort of men she had entertained when she was young. Not the sort she dallied with...or married.

By the time she reached the boarding house—she refused to give it so grand a name as hotel, which is what the owners called it—she still hadn't come to a firm conclusion about her next steps. In a town with more saloons than stores, she had few options.

Four women who'd arrived with her on the bride train were gathered in the front parlor, engaged in what appeared to be a somber discussion.

She hesitated by the door, imagining their reaction to her rather spontaneous decision to seek employment in a saloon. That wasn't her first choice, but she wasn't qualified for the usual jobs reserved for women, even if any were available. She could perform operas and quote Shakespeare, but she couldn't cook and didn't sew well enough to be a seamstress. In the traditional sense, she was inferior which was why it surprised her that the other women had accepted her so readily. They didn't know about her career. As soon as they found out, they would shun her. If she didn't go back to O'Shea's, she wouldn't have to tell them.

She stepped into the parlor. "Why the long faces?"

"We're discussing the latest ultimatum from Mr. Hardt." Susannah Braddock's stormy expression warned it was something ominous. If it involved the domineering railroad agent, that came as no surprise. "He's informed us the railroad will no longer pay for our room and board.

Dread pooled in the pit of Charm's stomach. She couldn't turn down a job if she would soon be homeless. "Most of the women who arrived with us are married, seven out of twelve. That doesn't make him happy?"

Susannah huffed. "He wants all of us married

yesterday. We are, in his words, taking advantage of his good will by dragging our feet in selecting suitors."

Hardt could be overbearing and unreasonable, but in Susannah's case, he might be right. The fair-haired widow had the perfect combination of angelic features and a body made for sin, as men would say. Educated, with homemaking skills as an added bonus, she had every man in town offering marriage—and she'd spurned all of them. She must have reasons for not wanting to marry although she continued to declare her intention to be wed when she found *the right man*.

Charm suspected a man didn't exist who would meet Susannah's exacting standards. As for herself, she wanted no man and nothing to do with marriage. Mr. Hardt would have to be satisfied with being compensated for her expenses, as soon as she had the money.

"Come join the discussion. We've been talking for over an hour and haven't come up with a solution." Prudence Walker shifted to make room on the sofa. If she had sat still for more than five minutes it would be amazing. She usually hopped from task to task, always busy, like an industrious wren. "You have good ideas, Charm. Help us resolve this dilemma."

"Put on a show to raise money." Charm surveyed the shocked reactions. "Bad idea?"

"I cannot believe he intends to throw us out." Delilah Bodean lifted her hand to her forehead in a dramatic gesture certain to bring a chivalrous man running—if one existed.

"Remember, Mr. Cold Heart tried to raffle us off the first day we arrived," Charm reminded her.

Delilah's sapphire eyes darkened with wounded confusion. "But he seemed to be thawing…"

"Spring on the heel of limping Winter treads," Charm recited.

The four women presented another round of blank stares.

She shrugged. "Shakespeare…I thought it apt."

With a sigh, she cradled her purse in her lap. She'd counted five dollars in tips, and in a generous mood had offered half to Mr. O'Shea. His unhappy reaction must mean he expected more. She would work harder and make more, and negotiate for a larger percentage because now she had to cover her living expenses, as well as pay what she owed the railroad and save enough to start over—preferably in a town with a theater or opera house. For now, she was stuck with working in a saloon. She would just have to make it clear to her employer that their relationship was strictly businesslike. If that wasn't already clear.

He'd certainly gotten his feathers ruffled when she asked to draw up an agreement. The idea came to her as an afterthought, remembering something her mother had told her once about not getting paid because of a misunderstanding. Mr. O'Shea's reaction made it clear he took umbrage at her suggestion, and when she tried to explain, she just made it worse. This was her first time to negotiate a business deal on her own. She wasn't even certain about what to write down besides the few details they had agreed on. With her luck, she would return only to find out that Mr. O'Shea had decided against hiring her.

"I might have an idea…" Hope Waverly perched on a stool in front of the piano. She liked to sit there, although she never played the instrument, or sang. Shyness?

Try as she might not to draw attention, she stood out like a blood red rose in a field of daisies. Her exotic features and dusky complexion hinted at mixed blood, which might account for her reticence. She feared being shunned.

Charm understood and sympathized. She encouraged Hope to express her opinion. "What's your idea?"

"We should ask Rose to talk to Mr. Hardt. He likes her."

That made sense. Rose, who was much too sweet for her own good, had managed to penetrate Mr. Hardt's tough hide. In a fit of jealousy, her beau had punched the railroad agent in the nose. Charm found the incident far more amusing than did the people involved.

"Good idea. Let's send in Rose to plead our case."

"No." Susannah shook her head, emphatically. "We don't need to cause trouble."

The whole town seethed with unrest. Men fought the railroad over land rights, fought with each other over women. In light of all that, what Hope suggested didn't sound so bad.

"I'm surprised the prospect of Mr. Hardt getting his nose punched again doesn't appeal to you."

A blush tinged Susannah's fair skin. Everyone knew about *the incident* between the outspoken young widow and the dour railroad agent. Charm just wished she had been there to see Susannah deliver the slap, or had at least heard it from the next room.

"It might be what he deserves, but I'm sure we can come up with something more effective on our own," Susannah said primly.

The other women glanced at each other with doubt. However, no one would naysay the self-appointed leader. Susannah had a kind heart and she meant well, which made her bossy mothering tolerable. Having a child must have stimulated her nurturing tendencies.

Charm noticed the precocious seven-year-old wasn't in his usual place at his mother's side. "Where's Danny?"

"He finished his school work, so I let him go play with his friends."

"That's good he's making friends." Charm looked around at the women who had become her friends and her drooping spirits lifted. They all came from different backgrounds, yet they had found a common bond in friendship. Rose even went so far as to call her *sister* after she had loaned the destitute young woman a pair of red garters on her wedding day. They jokingly referred to their tight-knit group as the Order of the Garter, a knightly sisterhood committed to each other's welfare.

Charm opened her purse and dumped the coins into her lap. She would help her friends. They would do no less for her. "This should be enough to pay for at least one day's rent. I'll have more after tomorrow."

Prudence gaped at the money. "Where did you get that?"

"It's half my tips. I'm starting a job at O'Shea's...as the star performer." That sounded better than saloon entertainer. "I went over there today and auditioned for the position Mr. O'Shea had advertised, and he hired me."

The bug-eyed looks were amusing, though not unexpected. Even so, she just offered to pay for their room and board. A *thank you* would've been nice.

"You can't be serious!" Prudence's outburst broke the awkward silence.

"Of course I'm serious. Does this...," Charm gestured at the pile of coins, "look like a joke?"

"But...but a *saloon?*" Prudence wrinkled her nose, leaving no question as to what she thought about such establishments.

The other ladies looked equally horrified.

"We can't take your money," Delilah declared.

"She means you shouldn't have to support us," Hope added quickly.

Her defense was unnecessary. What Delilah meant didn't matter. Charm chose to ignore the insult. "I don't

27

have to support us, I am *offering* to do so until we can work out different arrangements, or until you get married and move out."

"What about you?" Susannah asked. "You came out here to be married, too…or that's what you led us to believe."

The room grew warmer. Or was the heat due to the coals of guilt being heaped on her head? Charm removed her bonnet. She did feel bad about misleading her friends. But every woman in the room had secrets they weren't willing to tell. She was no different in that respect, and shouldn't be judged.

She scooped the coins into her purse. "Nothing prevents me from changing my mind."

"Only your word." Susannah delivered the pointed remark with the accuracy of a master archer. Her arrow pierced Charm's heart, and pain caused her to lash out.

"You're one to accuse. How many proposals have you had? Dozens? A hundred?"

Susannah's color rose. "No need to engage in hyperbole."

"My point is, you've haven't accepted one of them. At least I'm being honest about not wanting to be married, instead of leading everyone to believe I wish to be wed and then conveniently never making up my mind."

The other women's shocked expressions turned to frowning rebuke.

With her face burning, Charm turned and left without a word, not losing her composure until she reached the hall whereupon she lifted her skirts and fled up the stairs.

Why hadn't she held her tongue? She had no more right to chastise Susannah than Susannah had the right to chastise her. She expected too much from women who'd been brought up to look down on people like her. They couldn't be blamed for reacting as they did, and she shouldn't hold it against them, no matter how much their attitudes hurt.

She would still pay the rent, because it was the right thing to do.

Upstairs, she dragged one of her large suitcases from beneath the bed she shared with Prudence. Twelve women had arrived on the bride train to a town with only one hotel. They had been crammed into small bedrooms and forced to sleep together on beds meant for one. She wasn't sure how much the appalling lodging cost. Lodging wasn't something she had to worry about before, nor was food or transportation. Her mother had taken care of those things, and then Simon. Now that she was on her own, she had to be smarter and ask more questions.

Charm lifted the lid and began to remove her costumes to examine them for needed repairs.

A swish of skirts alerted her to the fact she wasn't alone.

"Why are you doing this, Charm?" Prudence asked.

Her bedmate couldn't help prying. She must've been bored living on a farm in Illinois because she took so much interest in everyone else's affairs. To her credit, she didn't gossip.

"I should think I made my reasons clear. I'm not interested in marriage, and I need a way support myself." Charm went back to sorting through her costumes, checking for tears, or heaven forbid, insect holes. The custom-made clothing represented a small fortune and her mother had taken great care to preserve the costumes in a cedar-lined trunk. The large trunk was too heavy for a quick escape, so a suitcase had to do. She made a mental note to find out where to purchase a cedar trunk so she could ensure her costumes would be well protected—yet another thing to worry about.

Prudence hovered behind her. "Please don't turn away. I'm not here to scold you. I-I just don't understand. Why would you give up the respectability of marriage to go to work in a saloon? The whole town will believe you're a…a…"

"An entertainer." Charm supplied the label, knowing full well it wasn't the one Prudence couldn't spit out. Her stammering attempt to converse about something she found uncomfortable would be funny, if it weren't insulting. "I will be singing and dancing and performing skits. That's all."

"That's *all?*" Another horrified look from Pru, this time without scrunching her nose. "Even stepping into a saloon can be ruinous to a woman's reputation, much less singing and dancing in one."

Charm tossed rainbow colored petticoats onto the bed. She couldn't expect Prudence, or any of the others reared in conventional families, to understand her Bohemian lifestyle. "This isn't the first time I've sung in a saloon." She didn't add that she hadn't performed in a place like O'Shea's since childhood, having advanced to opera houses and theaters. "The only reputation I care about is the one I'll establish by being the best at what I do best. Performing."

"I didn't know, you never told me."

There were a great many things she hadn't shared, in spite of being given the story of her friend's entire life. Sadly, it wasn't very entertaining.

"Some things are best kept to oneself."

Pru's eyes grew sad. "You'll never find a decent man to marry you if you take that job."

Continuing to pretend seemed pointless. Her parents' unhappy union had dampened Charm's enthusiasm for marriage. Her experience with Simon had put the nail in that coffin. "I don't need to find a decent man because I don't intend to be married."

"Then why did you answer the ad?"

Another somewhat spontaneous decision. Though Simon had given her no time to deliberate.

Charm ventured a confidence. "I had to escape someone who had too much power over me."

"Oh no." Prudence commenced to wringing her hands. "Don't tell me, you're already married and you're running from a husband."

"My sins aren't that great." Charm didn't expound. She dared not reveal everything, even to Prudence. One slip of the tongue and word could spread as faster than a cholera epidemic. Thus far, she'd told the other women she had traveled around the country and occasionally sang for people. Her story wasn't a lie, but it wasn't the full truth either. If her true identity got out, Simon would find her.

Fear coated her skin in ice. Simon had stolen more than her faith in others. To the world, he put on a good show of being caring and concerned. He had fooled her, too, for a time. She was wiser now, and would be on her guard against charming men...such as Mr. O'Shea.

"If you aren't married, you could be," Prudence insisted. "You're so pretty and smart and talented. All the men fawn over you. You'd have your pick of the litter."

Pick of the litter, a colorful way of putting it, and appropriate, if one considered men little more than beasts.

"I'll leave the men for you. You're the one who wants to be married so badly."

The moment the words left Charm's mouth, she regretted them. Her friend's golden brown eyes reflected surprise, and hurt. Prudence had reached her third decade unmarried and believed no one could want her. The thoughtless remark only reinforced her insecurities.

"I'm sorry, Pru. That was unkind. I don't know

what's gotten into me." Charm examined the tattered shawl in her hands, part of her costume when she played a servant girl dubbed Little Marchioness. She could make herself look attractive, as well as look like an old hag. She could play any part, except her true self. She didn't know that part anymore.

Charm forced herself to look her friend in the eye. "The truth is, you are as attractive as I am. Actually, more so, because you hide your natural gifts and I enhance mine. I don't have your womanly figure. Without all the padding, and my face powders, eye kohl and lip stain, I look rather plain."

"Oh pshaw, you couldn't look plain if you tried...and you don't have to flatter me. I know what I look like, I've seen my face in the mirror." Prudence smoothed her hands over a stained apron. Flour caked the edges of her fingernails. The poor woman spent all her time in the kitchen, helping out. No wonder she hadn't found a husband.

"You shouldn't let Mrs. Fry take advantage of you."

Prudence shrugged. "I like to cook, and I'm counting on a man noticing my skills."

Charm had to admit her friend's plan seemed sounder than hers thus far. "Once some handsome farmer gets a bite of your sausage gravy and biscuits, it'll be love at first sight...I mean, bite."

Amusement eased the tension. Charm returned to sorting costumes. "Thank you for coming up here to check on me."

"Everyone's concerned. We all love you..."

Loved her? That couldn't be true. They'd sat there looking at her with condemnation in their eyes. Or had she only seen what she expected?

"That's why we don't want you to leave."

Where did Pru think she would go? To live over the saloon with Mr. O'Shea? The image brought on a warm flush far too pleasant to be proper. "I'll be living here, so don't get your hopes up about having a bed to yourself. Right now, I'm just checking my costumes, in case any need repairs."

Prudence eyed the gowns with longing. "The dresses are so pretty...and the petticoats."

None of them would fit her, or Charm would've offered one. Her friend's drab clothing selection and severe hairstyles didn't do her justice. "Would you like to help me select what to wear for my debut performance?"

"What about this one?" Prudence lifted a snow-white dress made of silk with a tulle overlay.

Charm's stomach knotted. That was her mother's favorite, too. For different reasons.

"La Belle Enfant. The name fits you, my dear. You look so young. So innocent. When you wear this dress, especially. You stir men's protective urges. Make them feel heroic. At the same time, they burn to possess you. This is your power. Use it to your advantage."

The white dress had made her famous, so she couldn't dispute its effectiveness. Much as she hated it, she wasn't responsible for the dichotomy of men's emotions toward innocent girls. As Mama had so frankly stated, she was giving them what they wanted.

Maybe that was why Simon had assumed she would welcome his advances.

Charm frowned at the disturbing thought. "That one will get dirty." She wouldn't wear it regardless. Someone might recognize her in the signature costume. "Saloons aren't the cleanest places."

"I imagine not. How can you stand being around drunken men?" Prudence scrunched her nose. That bad smell again.

Charm had grown up over her father's saloon in San Francisco. Back then, she hadn't known any different. "I suppose I'm used to it."

"What will you do if the men…lose control?"

"Assault me, you mean?" She didn't add that the only man who had assaulted her wasn't drunk. She would use a portion of her earnings to purchase a pistol in case he caught up with her. "I trust Mr. O'Shea won't allow me to come to harm."

"How can you be sure? You don't know him."

Why she felt secure with the brawny Irishman, Charm couldn't say. "If I see reason to doubt, I'll find another way to protect myself."

Prudence draped the white dress on the bed with a reverence that made Charm flinch. White stood for purity and innocence. Charm could claim neither.

"You're set on it, then," Pru said softly. "There's nothing I can say to talk you out of it?"

The die had been cast long ago. Charm knew no other life, nor did she want a different one. She shook her head. "No. Nothing."

Chapter Three

Patrick woke early the next morning in an optimistic mood. Even the stiffness in his muscles didn't seem as bad, or maybe it just didn't bother him as much because his thoughts were occupied with visions of his good luck charm.

That would be a good stage name. He would suggest it when he met with Miss LaBelle to hammer out an agreement. As much as he despised the impersonal nature of contracts, he could see the value. Once word got around about her astonishing talent, the other saloon owners would try to hire her away. Having her signature on a legal document would protect his interests.

Hobbling to the dresser, he picked up a small pill and rolled it between his fingers. Each morning, he'd crush the opium into the bottom of a glass and mix the bitter medicine with sugared whiskey. The stuff would work its magic and he'd be able to move with less pain. But over time, he found he needed more to get the same relief. The more he took, the slower his mind worked.

He put down the pill. He could do without the medicine this morning, and if he made it through tomorrow, he might find he didn't need it anymore. By the time he dressed and ate his usual breakfast, oat porridge liberally doused with honey, he felt much better.

Before he left his room, he stopped in front of a small statue standing serenely on a shelf beside the door. His mother had tucked the icon into his knapsack before he'd left Ireland, assuring him it would bring him luck. After his brother was killed, he'd put the statue away. Last night, the Virgin Mary had reclaimed her place of honor. He still doubted his prayers reached past the ceiling, and wondered if there was anything more than clouds in the heavens, but he wasn't so certain that he'd pitch his religion out the window. Indeed, what had happened yesterday was nothing less than a miracle.

He made the sign of the cross. "Blessed Mary, I thank you for bringing me a good luck charm..." He hesitated. Normally, he'd confess to a priest, but there wasn't one handy, and he felt the need to make amends. "Forgive me for putting you in the sock drawer."

Patrick took care descending the stairs. For some reason, going down was worse than climbing up. One wrong step would send his back into spasms, or aggravate the pain in his hip. By the time he reached the bottom, he'd broken out in a sweat even though the air felt cool.

The inside of the saloon remained dim, the only light coming through a window in the front. He propped open the door to bring in more light and air the place out, so it didn't reek. He'd gotten used to the odors, but Miss LaBelle might not like it. On the other hand, she'd strolled in and demanded a job, so the smell must not bother her overmuch.

After he donned his apron, he took a clean rag and wiped down the bar. My, but Charm had astonished him when she'd climbed up and started singing. She possessed beauty, a sweet voice and a rare talent for captivating a crowd. Every man in the room had become her devoted swain.

Including him.

His smile faded. Only a fool would fall for her act. Women who loved to charm men couldn't be satisfied with just one. Even her name should be a warning. Ruminating on the sobering thought, Patrick dusted bottles on the shelves. A more cheerful prospect, the money he would earn while she worked for him. He could expand the saloon, maybe purchase billiards tables. At the sound of footsteps, he turned, feather duster in hand, ridiculously eager. When he saw who stood in the doorway, his anticipation fled.

"Mr. Hardt. Good morning."

"The same to you, O'Shea. Though whether it's good remains to be seen." Hardt moved toward the bar with purposeful strides. A fair bet the land agent wasn't here for a drink. He didn't fraternize with the clientele. Even if he were social, the settlers would dislike him purely on the basis of his association with the railroad and its rich owner, who'd stolen the land out from under them. Being standoffish didn't help Hardt's cause, though. The settlers thought he considered himself above them and was out of touch with problems faced by the common man. Hardt didn't dress like them, either. He wore three-piece suits, black or gray, never opting for trousers in popular stripes or paisley. Today, his black suit fit the look on his face.

Patrick hung the feather duster beside the shelf. He rested his arm on the bar and shifted his weight off his bad leg. "Something I can do for you?" he inquired politely.

"Tell me you didn't hire Miss LaBelle."

Hardt acted awfully proprietary about a woman he'd been ready to raffle off.

"'Fraid I can't do that. She starts today."

"She has a contract with the railroad."

"Does she now?" Patrick strove to keep the irritation out of his voice. A signature on a piece of paper was only as good a man's word—or a woman's in this case. If Charm didn't keep her word on the deal she made with the railroad, he had no reason to believe she'd keep her word to him; and to think she had the nerve to ask him to sign something, as if *his* honor was in question. He'd have a talk with her about this other contract when she showed up.

"Miss LaBelle signed an agreement to be wed. In return, her fare, room and board were covered." Hardt acted like the inequity of the arrangement had never struck him.

"You bought her that cheap?" Patrick's quip didn't elicit a smile. Maybe Hardt didn't have a sense of humor. Though he'd made a fool out of that stupid hothead Jarvis, who'd wagered away his land. In that instance, the railroad agent demonstrated wisdom and a keen sense of fairness. Pray he would show the same levelheaded thinking in the case of a runaway bride.

"Miss LaBelle will be performing tonight, if you'd like to stop by and see her." Patrick didn't mention Charm's imminent arrival. Wouldn't want Hardt spoiling his good fortune.

"You cannot hire these women we brought in," the agent said bluntly.

Patrick's hackles went up at being told what to do. He'd resented orders while in the army; and he sure as hell didn't answer to a former Union officer who'd probably bought his post. How else would a southerner get to be a U.S. major? "Last time I checked, it was a free country. We made sure of it when we whipped the Rebs."

Hardt crossed his arms over his chest. "I didn't fight for your right to corrupt decent women."

The irritation prickling Patrick's skin became a slow burn. "Mr. Hardt. Yer gettin' awfully close to insulting me." His brogue thickened the angrier he got. "Fer the sake of keepin' the peace, I'll let it pass this time. Miss LaBelle came in here, she asked for a job, and I gave her one. If you got a complaint, I suggest you take it up with her. But don't come in here again and try to tell me what I can or can't do."

Some emotion flickered in Hardt's eyes, not anger, more like grudging respect. He dropped the defensive stance. "My intention isn't to insult you, O'Shea. If you don't care about the legal implications, then I must ask you, as a gentleman, to consider the consequences of this decision. If you employ that young lady, she might as well announce that she's entertaining customers."

Patrick entertained the idea of wrapping his fingers around Hardt's neck, and would have if the agent had been expressing a singular opinion. He only echoed what society in general believed. "Not all women who sing in saloons and work in dance halls are prostitutes."

"Try convincing the men who come in here."

Patrick stiffened with anger. Pain radiated from hip down his right leg. He remained straight through sheer willpower. "Nobody, including you, will abuse Miss LaBelle as long as she's under my protection."

"Then I'd suggest you bring her under your protection permanently. Marry her."

"Marry her?" Patrick repeated it because he was sure he hadn't heard right.

Hardt nodded. "It would solve a number of problems."

And introduce a host of others.

"That's not possible."

Disappointment flickered across the agent's face. "If you won't make her respectable then let another man have her."

Patrick refused the bait. He wouldn't be bullied into marriage. "She knows what she's getting into."

"She might. I'm not sure you do." Hardt withdrew a folded paper from inside his coat. "Are you aware of an earlier claim on this property?"

The agent shouldn't play poker with such an obvious bluff.

"There's no one else who can make a legitimate claim on this land and you know it."

"No one other than the man who built here first."

"Gilly?" Patrick laughed. Talk about reaching for straws. His friend, an old army chum, had come out here and put up a sod building, but he hadn't liked living in the wilds and swore he wouldn't return. "He sold me his place. We shook on it. Gilly wouldn't go back on his word."

"Mr. McGill sold you a sod structure. He didn't own the land beneath it. But he and his brother filed a claim together, and it's dated before the one you filed. See for yourself." Hardt unfolded the paper and pushed it across the bar. "Mr. McGill arrived in town yesterday. He's contesting your ownership and wants me to assign him rights."

Patrick examined the signatures. He wouldn't know his friend's mark, having never seen it. There were two names, two McGills, on the claim. Worry churned in his stomach. He pushed the paper back to Hardt. "Well, there's a simple solution. Just ask Gilly. He'll tell you he sold me the soddy and intended that to include the land."

"Mr. McGill died several months ago and left everything to his brother, who says he knew nothing about the deal."

Patrick had to pound something, so he pounded his fist on the bar. "Then he's a liar!"

Hardt didn't bat an eye. "He's presented a valid claim that predates the one you filed."

Furious, Patrick paced. He favored his aching leg, the pain worsening as his anger escalated. He couldn't lose this place, not now, and not to a cheat. "Gilly's an honest man. He would've given his brother half the proceeds he made on the sale. You ought to realize this. You picked up on a cheater's lie before with Jarvis, and you did the right thing when he tried to cheat Val. Do the right thing now. Assign the land to me, instead of letting that lying whelp steal it."

The stone-faced agent seemed to consider his plea, if silence was any indication. "I'm not unsympathetic, but McGill has a valid claim...and he's a married man. You aren't. Railroad directives require me to assign claims first to married men."

The muscles in Patrick's back clenched. He halted, unable to walk without excruciating pain. This couldn't be happening. Not now. Not when it seemed his life had finally taken a turn for the better. He'd put everything he owned into this business. Coming out here to pursue what he'd been sure was a better life had cost him dearly. He refused to give up without a fight.

Only, this fight would end up in court in an expensive battle. Judges always sided with rich men and the railroads. Again, Luck had played a cruel trick on him.

"If you were to marry Miss LaBelle, it would be easier for me to make an argument that you should retain rights to the land, based on your previous agreement and your improvements. Think about it." Hardt touched his hat brim. "I'll leave you to your preparations. Good day."

Think about it.

The agent had offered a solution, and oh, how simple and convenient he made it sound.

Patrick closed his eyes and took deep breaths, trying to relax.

He could keep his saloon if he married Charm.

God, he was tempted.

41

What rot had crawled into his brain? She had her pick from more than a hundred men, most of them healthier, but she hadn't come in here looking for a marriage proposal. If she wanted to be wed, she wouldn't be asking for a job. He'd have no luck on that account.

Pain stabbed his hip and lower back as the abused muscles twisted into knots. He gasped and shifted his stance. That only worsened the spasms. His legs trembled. In minute, he'd be on his knees. Bracing his hands on the bar, he used the strength in his arms to support his weight. Now wasn't the time for his body to give out. Not when he had a fight to wage against those who would try to take everything away from him.

"Mr. O'Shea!" Charm rushed to her new employer's side. She'd seen the frowning railroad agent exit the saloon and to avoid having to deal with him, she hid behind the side of the building until he crossed the street. When she'd reached the open door, Mr. O'Shea had been hunched over, gasping, clinging to the bar for support.

She wrapped her arms around him, praying she could hold him up long enough to assist him to a chair. "What's wrong? Did Mr. Hardt attack you?"

He gave a harsh laugh, neither confirmation nor denial. The muscles in his abdomen tensed as he released another labored breath. Hanging his head, he stared downward, seeming to put all his energy into concentrating. If he fell, he'd take her down with him. Regardless, she wouldn't let go and allow him to crumple.

"Here, I'll help you to a chair."

"Leave me be," he muttered.

What was it about men that made them refuse help when they so obviously needed it? He'd be more embarrassed if he ended up in a heap on the floor.

She moved around to one side and kept her arm about his waist. He felt so strong, so solid. Her heart ached at seeing him trembling in distress. "Please tell me how I can be of assistance."

He shifted, leaning his weight to one side, away from her. He wasn't in any condition to push her away, nor did she want him to, oddly enough. She longed to hold him and reassure him.

Where had *that* come from? She wasn't a particularly compassionate person. Yet, it wasn't compassion, exactly, that she felt. Protective? That made no sense, either. She hardly knew him, and the thought of her protecting a big man like Patrick O'Shea was laughable. Maybe that's why he laughed when she first put her arms around him.

A fine sheen of perspiration glistened on his forehead. His black brows gathered in a fierce frown and pain darkened his eyes.

"You look terrible."

His throat worked, dark amusement crossed his face. "I feel terrible."

"Then you need to sit down instead of being bullheaded about accepting my help."

"I'm not so weak I have to be helped to a chair like an old man." He reached for an unmarked bottle on a shelf beneath the bar. His hands shook as he poured a measured amount of reddish liquid in a glass.

Charm had grown up with a man who required a drink every morning just to get out of bed. Her father's tremors came on when he didn't get his whiskey. Was that what was wrong with Mr. O'Shea?

What did it matter whether he liked his liquor? She would only be working for him. As long as he treated her right and paid her on time, what he did was none of her business.

He downed the drink in one gulp. Afterwards, he stood with his hands braced on the bar, as if waiting for something. In few moments, his breathing slowed. "That'll help."

She eyed the glass. "I know whiskey is considered a cure-all, but I'm not convinced."

He released a heavy breath. *What butter or whiskey does not cure cannot be cured.* So say the old folks."

"Did it help them?"

He shrugged.

At least he seemed more in control. Her father had needed an entire glassful of whiskey in the morning, not just a shot.

As the crisis passed, she became aware she had her hand on her employer's arm. Warmth seeped through the fabric of his shirt. His body radiated heat. Any woman fortunate enough to curl up beside him at night would never be cold.

She jerked her hand away, startled by the direction her mind had wandered. She had no desire to curl up beside Mr. O'Shea, or any other man, for that matter.

He straightened, slowly, and was soon back to acting self-confident, although he appeared wrung out. "Better now. Just a wee pain."

His attempt to downplay the frightening episode was really quite endearing.

"A wee pain? I'd hate to see what a severe pain might do to you." Without thinking, she withdrew her handkerchief from beneath her sleeve, reached up and mopped the sweat on his brow.

Based on his stunned expression, she'd surprised him—almost as much as she surprised herself. She withdrew her hand. His heat had magically transferred to her face. She focused her attention on folding the handkerchief. "What brought it on, this wee pain?"

He didn't answer right away.

She lifted her head and their eyes met. The tension in the air fairly crackled, humming energy that started up whenever they were in close proximity.

His gaze became thoughtful. "Mr. Hardt paid me a visit this morning."

"Did he?" She hesitated, apprehensive. The railroad agent might've heard she'd taken a job and tried to thwart her. "What did he want?"

"He mentioned you have a contract. With the railroad. Something you didn't tell me." Mr. O'Shea's tone wasn't scolding, but she sensed his disappointment nonetheless.

"The paper I signed? That doesn't mean I'm their slave. They can't force me to marry."

He frowned at her response. "No one can force you to do anything you don't want to."

Want had nothing to do with it. She longed to find someone to love and to be loved in return. Except, marriage required her to give up control. Having been at the mercy of a man who wasn't her husband was bad enough. Married, she would have no way out. If she tried to explain her feelings to Mr. O'Shea, he would laugh at her, or think she was crazy.

"Mr. Hardt is worried about losing money. I'll make restitution from my earnings."

Her employer braced his hand on the bar. Despite his bravado, he still showed signs of being shaky. "I'll cover whatever you owe."

Oh no, she would not be obligated. That was just another snare. "You don't have to pay my debts."

"Less trouble for both of us if it's done and out of the way. If it makes you feel better, I'll take a little out of your pay each week 'til we're even."

He was being generous, which in her experience

made him suspect. People didn't extend favors without wanting one in return. He had a point, though. If Mr. Hardt's financial concerns were satisfied, the agent would be less likely to make trouble for her.

"I'll consider your offer." She gestured to a table, having the perfect excuse to get him to a chair. "If you're ready to negotiate our agreement, why don't we sit down? You can pour us each a drink. I'll take a brandy."

His eyebrows arched. He would be even more surprised if she asked for a cigar. Something she had tried and not found to her liking. To her relief, he didn't rebuke her. Instead, he took down a bottle and poured her a drink.

As an actress, she had long been exiled from *proper* society, which held that men could enjoy whiskey and cigars, while women were allowed only medicinal tonics for female complaints. Ironically, the ingredients in tonics were fermented in alcohol or liberally laced with opium. She avoided them, having seen too many of her friends become dependent on daily doses, and their health seemed to grow worse, not better.

Mr. O'Shea followed her to a nearby table. He pulled out her chair, set the drink in front of her and then sank heavily into the chair opposite. His stiff movements indicated he still suffered from whatever ailment had debilitated him earlier. The "wee pain" must be why he limped, and today the limp appeared worse. No wonder he turned to whiskey.

"You aren't having anything?" she asked.

"I've had all I need."

She couldn't remember a time her father had refused whiskey. Perhaps her employer didn't overindulge because he'd observed the ill effects, or didn't wish to drink away his profit.

The strong scent of apples teased her nose. This didn't

smell like her favorite brandy. After her last show in Chicago, one of the gentlemen in the audience had sent her a bottle of Hennessy Cognac. She released a wistful sigh. There could be no returning to that life. Not right away.

"Would you happen to have French Cognac?"

"Not at the moment. I'll be sure to find some, now that I know your preferences." Mr. O'Shea's firm lips twitched into a half-smile. She wished to see his face without all that facial hair, but mentioning it would imply she found him fascinating.

"Merci," she murmured, smiling as she took a sip. The brandy turned into liquid fire in her mouth, so strong she could hardly swallow it. She set the glass down, took a breath and blew it out. "Stronger than I'm used to…"

"You might prefer wine." His expression remained bland, although she spotted a mischievous gleam in his eyes.

"Perhaps later." She didn't wish to be the only one drinking. That would put her at a disadvantage when negotiating. He obviously knew it, and that would explain why he'd served her Fire Water. "What do you propose to pay me?

"A dollar a day, plus twenty-five percent on tips."

If he knew with whom he bargained—one of the most sought after actresses in the country—he would know he'd just insulted her. But no, she couldn't think like that. As far as he was concerned, she was an unknown hopeful who'd wandered into his saloon. There was no reason, however, to allow him to assume he bartered with a pea brain.

"I'll keep the tips. If you require more than the enormous profit you stand to make on drinks, we can charge an admission and split the income."

He leaned his arms on the table, holding her gaze. "Men don't pay to get into a saloon."

His reply gave her a marvelous idea.

"Turn your saloon into a theater. Then they'll pay admission." She sat back and gestured broadly with her hands. "This building is large enough. You could put a stage at one end. I could find someone to help me paint the canvas backdrops. We'll need stage lights…kerosene is too smoky. Limelight would be best."

"A theater." He didn't look enthusiastic. She thought it a grand idea.

"Look at it this way, you'll have something none of your competitors offer."

Working in a theater would also blunt expectations that she would mingle with patrons, sit on their laps and encourage drinking. She could hardly bear being close to men, much less allowing them to paw her.

"Make it nice enough and you could attract big stars…" *Like me.* Tempting as it was, sharing her true identity would be too risky. "Like Jack Langrishe or Lydia Thompson."

Her employer folded his arms over his chest. "Build a theater big enough to attract the likes of those two? Out here? That's shooting awfully high."

His remark puzzled her because it never occurred to her to aim low. She appealed to his vanity. "Not if you're a man of vision."

Regret flickered in his eyes before he shuttered his emotions behind a frank look. "You'll find visions don't take you very far out here, Miss LaBelle. Take my advice, be practical."

Perhaps she expected too much. He wasn't as ambitious as she hoped, or he didn't give a woman's opinion much credence. That didn't mean she would give up.

"Mr. O'Shea, if I was practical, I wouldn't have come in here and asked for a job."

Chapter Four

The saloon remained closed the following morning so Patrick could build a platform for his new performer. Miss LaBelle wanted more. Something bigger and better than anything he could possibly provide. Just like Kathleen. She hadn't been satisfied with her lot, either.

Charm dreamed bigger dreams. When she talked about building a theater and bringing in big stars illuminated in limelight, her eyes glowed. Ah, but it sounded so grand and glorious. The kind of crazy idea he might've pursued when he was younger. Before life had taught him not to reach so high. He settled for smaller dreams now, because he couldn't bear to want too much and have it taken away.

For a moment, he'd considered asking her to marry him...until she'd declared, with much vehemence, her opposition to marriage. He would have to find another way to keep his land. Bribery? He barely had enough to cover expenses.

Patrick swung the hammer, taking out his frustration on a nail. He couldn't dismantle the building and move it. Even if he could manage such a feat, all the town sites had been claimed.

While he stewed and hammered, Charm chattered on, ignorant of the struggle he waged.

She had arrived at half past ten, thirty minutes late. When he reminded her that she would need to be prompt, she informed him she wasn't a morning person, as if that was supposed to excuse her for being tardy. He didn't give a tinker's damn if she disliked mornings as long as she showed up for her performances. He wasn't putting that in writing, though. Let her stew over it.

He paid little attention to the rough sketch of a stage she provided. How hard could it be to build a platform? Instead of leaving him to it, she remained to offer instruction, which he didn't need. He wouldn't have minded her company if she'd sit down and talk to him. Whenever she ventured near, she would flitter away, reminding him of a hummingbird.

"You should think about adding a chandelier. Mr. McGuire's New Opera House in Virginia City is three stories high, with six gas chandeliers made from Austrian crystal, and gas footlights, and a double tier of boxes draped in scarlet, and gilt chairs and velvet railing…"

She sounded very familiar with the place.

"You've been there I take it?"

Silence. For the first time in the past hour…

"Do you think this stage is large enough? It needs to be at least six feet deep."

Either she had the attention span of a hummingbird, or she had changed the subject on purpose.

Charm whisked around his right side just as he lifted the hammer. The flash of a slender ankle and a whiff of perfume distracted him. He struck his thumb instead of the nail.

"Bloody hell!" Sitting back on his heels, he gripped

the wounded digit and bit his lip to keep from releasing a torrent of obscenities. Throbbed like the very devil.

"I can't concentrate with you hovering over my shoulder," he muttered.

She retreated in a swirl of violet skirts.

Patrick cursed his vile temper. Wasn't her fault he was a clumsy oaf. If he'd kept his mind on his work instead of how good she smelled and how pretty she looked, and how much he wanted things he had no business wanting, he wouldn't have hammered his thumb.

He turned with an apology on his lips.

"Here…" She thrust a glass of whiskey at him.

Kind of her, and she didn't appear offended by his rudeness. His wife would've dissolved into tears if he'd snapped at her like that

Patrick offered a contrite smile. "Thanks, but I don't need a drink."

"It's for your thumb, silly. Soak it. It'll help."

Drinking the stuff would help more. Though if he downed a glassful of whisky on top of the medicine, he wouldn't be able to see the nail, much less strike it.

He dipped his thumb in the glass. Winced as it started to burn. Blood turned the reddish liquid darker.

"Good heavens, you're bleeding!" Off she went, and snatched a small towel hanging on a hook beneath the front of the bar. He started to remind her that men wiped beer off their mustaches with that, but she was already back, tearing the towel in half.

She looked pointedly at his injured hand. With a sigh, he held up his thumb and she proceeded to wrap it. She fussed over him more than his sainted mother. Somebody needed to marry the girl and give her a flock of children.

Patrick jerked his hand away.

She blinked with surprise.

"I'll take care of it," he explained. No sense encouraging her to give him the wrong idea. At least she wasn't shying away from him. Maybe he seemed less threatening injured. But if he did something stupid like proposing, she'd dart out the door and never return. Not only that, it wouldn't be fair to marry her just because he needed a wife to keep his land. She deserved better

He tried to hold a nail, couldn't get his thumb around it with the unwieldy bandage. "The stage can't be any bigger. It's already taken up five feet. We need room for the customers."

She crossed her arms and her lower lip curled out. When he didn't respond to her pout, she dropped the act. "Oh, all right. I'll make do with five feet. But don't forget about the ropes."

He looked up at the stamped tin ceiling, apprehensive. She wanted him to drive large hooks into the floor joists and had described some acrobatic feat where she would "fly" across the heads of the patrons. Scared him to death just thinking about it. What if the rope broke and she fell, or one of those stupid tracklayers jumped up on a table and hauled her out of the air, or worse, some drunken settler fired off a gun in a frenzy of excitement.

Patrick got to his feet, fighting a strong urge to haul her into his arms and protect her from her own crazy self. "That sounds dangerous. Why don't you just sing?"

She cocked her head and looked at him like he'd said something stupid. "After hours of singing, I'd be hoarse. I wouldn't be able to sing the next night. Besides, variety will add spice."

He could think of a few other things that would add *spice*, but he wouldn't want her doing them in front of anyone but him. "You said you played the banjo."

"Yes, I'll play and dance and perform skits. I know several amusing variations on Shakespeare." Again came the sigh. "But I've always wanted to fly across a room."

His heart jerked in his chest. "You mean you've never done it?"

"Not exactly…" She glanced off to one side, as if meeting his eyes made her uncomfortable. "How hard can it be? Adah Menken performed *Mazeppa* tied naked to a horse."

Appalled, Patrick grabbed her arm, pulled her over and covered her mouth. "Hush up, now. No more talk about flying or riding naked. You can do your act with your clothes on—and both feet on the ground."

His palm tingled from the pressure of her soft lips, and in his head a fantasy formed involving other places she might put them. A sudden heaviness in his groin signaling arousal shook him out of the trance. He took his hand away and released her. One good thing, the pain in his thumb had become inconsequential.

She stared at him like he'd grown horns. Her lips parted, but nothing came out. Apparently, he'd rendered her mute, the woman who never stopped talking.

Patrick turned away before he made a bigger fool of himself by doing something idiotic, like kissing her. He knelt in front of the partially completed stage and picked up his hammer. He would finish the stage, concentrate on that, and remember she was only an employee.

He attacked a nail with vigor. *Pound, pound.* He would not kiss her. *Pound, pound.* He would not propose. *Pound, pound.* He gave the nail one last ferocious pounding.

"I think you've got that one in good." She inched closer. Her tantalizing scent filled his nostrils and lust nearly overwhelmed him.

He threw an irritated look over his shoulder. If he didn't get rid of her, she would notice his reaction, or cause him to bust up his other fingers. "You plan to stand there all day watchin' me?"

She drew back looking hurt. "I'm not watching you. I'm overseeing construction. But if you find my presence annoying, I'll go fetch my costumes."

Turning on her heel, she left.

Patrick removed the rag from around his thumb, which had soaked up the blood but made it impossible to work. He released a heavy sigh. Finally, he managed to offend her. She wouldn't accept a proposal now...even if he worked up the courage to offer one.

By the time Charm reached the hotel, she was over being put out with her employer. She tucked away a reminder not to try Mr. O'Shea's very limited patience. This included doing ridiculous things like nursing his injuries and hovering over him just to be close. In the future, she would keep her distance. Proximity stirred confusing emotions, the kind she wasn't prepared to deal with now...if ever.

Upon entering the hotel, she noticed the quiet. Normally, sounds of conversation and laughter filled the rooms downstairs. She passed by the first doorway. None of her friends lounged in the parlor. Crossing the empty dining room, she peeked into the kitchen.

At a worktable, the proprietor's wife patted a ball of dough and picked up a rolling pin. Steam rose from a cast iron pot atop the stove.

Savory smells triggered grumbles from Charm's empty stomach. "Umm. Are you preparing pot pies?" The flaky pastries stuffed with chicken and vegetables were her favorite.

Mrs. Fry twisted around, looking surprised. "Oh, Miss LaBelle. I didn't hear you come in." The older woman set aside the rolling pin and wiped her hands on her apron. Her gaze darted away, communicating discomfort.

How strange. Usually she was friendly and very chatty.

Charm's instincts quivered like a divining rod sensing water. "Where is everyone?"

"They've gone to visit Mrs. Valentine."

That wasn't a disaster. Although it did seem a bit odd, considering her friends hadn't mentioned the excursion earlier. They might've known she would like to go along. She hadn't seen Rose in over a week. She released a sigh, and crossed to the cookstove. Using a dishtowel hanging over the handle on the oven door, she lifted the lid on the pot and sniffed the creamy mixture. *Heavenly.* "I wish they'd waited on me."

"They weren't sure you'd be returning."

"Not returning? Why would they think that?"

"We heard you were leaving."

The lid clanged as Charm dropped it on top of the pot. She'd gotten distracted by the food. That must be why this conversation didn't make sense. "Leaving? I'm just starting a job."

"Yes, well, Mr. Fry assumed you would be moving out." Mrs. Fry's tone seemed a mite cool. They must be worried about not getting paid.

"I don't know where he got that impression, but I plan to stay; and what's more, I'll have enough money to cover our room and board."

That should've made the old woman happy. Her frown deepened, sending a warning. "I am sorry, dear. Mr. Fry worked out an arrangement with the others. They'll be moving to a room on the third floor and helping us out. You understand why we can't offer the same arrangement to you, what with you working in a saloon. That would be bad for business."

The sanctimonious old witch picked up the rolling pin and went back to work on the dough.

Charm's stomach churned again, this time with

anger. She had dealt with scorn before. But to be kicked out set a new low, and to toss her out while her friends weren't around…utterly craven. Come to think of it, her friends should be here, supporting her.

Unease prickled her skin. "Do the others know you're evicting me?"

Mrs. Fry paused in her work without meeting Charm's eyes. "They thought it would be best if they weren't around when you returned. Less embarrassing for you."

The betrayal tore a hole through Charm's heart.

Too hurt and humiliated to argue, she left the kitchen and went upstairs. She'd change for the performance, pack her bags and leave. Even if the other women changed their minds and begged her to return, she would not. She wouldn't remain friends with people who could abandon her because her choices embarrassed them.

For once in her life, she'd risked putting her faith in people outside of her close circle. Desperately lonely, aching for companionship, she hadn't seen the falseness in their friendship.

She wouldn't give her trust again so easily.

Charm lugged the heavy suitcases down the sidewalk, ignoring the men who passed by in wagons and on horseback, especially those who called out to get her attention. She could more than imagine what they wanted.

The weight of the cases dragged her shoulders lower. Tightening her hold on the leather handles, she kept her eyes trained on a quadrangle of businesses that formed the heart of town: Appleton's mercantile, Middaugh's dry goods store, a blacksmith and livery, and the largest building, the railroad depot. Other stores lined the sidewalks, as well as numerous saloons, which were the only places besides the hotel that rented out rooms—for men. Women didn't take rooms above saloons unless they were engaged in the oldest business in the world.

Charm's spirits sank. Where she could find a room, she had no idea, but that was something she would have to figure out later. She had a show to put on first.

The sound of creaking wheels came from behind. Out of the side of her eye she spotted a harnessed horse. My, but it was a big one. Her head didn't come up to the top of the creature's shoulder, and its feathered hooves looked the size of plates. The dappled gray monster plodded closer to the sidewalk, so close she feared it might step on her.

Alarmed, she jerked out of the way.

"Whoa now." At the driver's order, the horse came to a halt, let out a loud snort and shook its thick white mane. The man's apologetic smile showed from beneath the shadow of a straw hat. "Sorry Miss. Sadie didn't mean to scare you. We thought you might need a ride someplace."

Charm eyed the brawny young farmer who'd nearly run her over and had the nerve to blame a dumb beast. "The horse told you that?"

He grinned, revealing white teeth with a slight gap between the front. "Sophie don't have to talk. Just nods her head and I know what she means."

"A creative excuse, I'll give you that."

"Pardon me, miss. You must think I'm a hayseed without any manners at all. Arch Childers, at your service." He swept off his hat and executed a bow worthy of Edwin Booth. As he straightened, he threw his head to toss his shoulder-length auburn hair out of his eyes.

The young farmer had a certain rustic appeal, even though he didn't make her heart pound. Not like Mr. O'Shea. Charm scoffed at the fanciful notion. The Irish saloon owner wasn't the only man in the world who could send her heart racing. There were others...she just hadn't met them.

"May we give you a ride?" Mr. Childers indicted the buckboard seat.

Charm hesitated. She wasn't in the habit of accepting an escort from men she didn't know, and the idea of getting into a wagon with a stranger made her palms clammy. On the other hand, a stranger hadn't assaulted her, and the alternative would be to drag her bags another three blocks through the mud.

A first step in getting rid of her unseemly infatuation for Mr. O'Shea would be to allow other men to assist her. She bestowed a smile on the helpful Galahad. "Thank you, sir. I accept your offer."

With an eager smile, he hopped down and tossed both suitcases into the back of the wagon as if they weighed no more than a woman's reticule. He secured them with ropes on top of a heavy canvas covering what looked like large boxes.

When he offered his hand, she took it. That didn't produce a thrill, either. She refused to think about the shivers elicited by Mr. O'Shea's touch.

She must fight this irrational attraction and keep her goal in mind. As soon as she repaid her debt to the railroad and saved enough money to start over, she would go further west, maybe to Virginia City. With a new identity.

Mr. Childers circled the wagon, gave the ropes holding her bags one last tug, and then hopped up onto the seat. He gathered the reins. "Where to?"

"O'Shea's." Charm braced for a look of surprise, or worse, censure. She received neither. Instead, her benefactor smiled.

"What do you know? That's where I'm headed."

Chapter Five

Patrick peered in the mirror behind the bar and rubbed his fingers over his smooth shaven chin. He hadn't seen his face in so long he'd forgotten what he looked like. Wasn't missing anything.

He adjusted his tie, smoothing the black points down, and brushed lint off the shawl collar of his favorite waistcoat, a dark green brocade. He thought it only appropriate to wear a suit for Charm's debut.

Where was she anyway?

With a tug on the fob, he pulled up his watch and consulted the time. The hotel wasn't far. Shouldn't take her half the day to collect a few costumes.

She might be staying away on purpose after he'd snapped at her, and for something that wasn't her fault. His attraction to her. That, he couldn't control, but he could curb his temper. When she arrived, he would be on his best behavior, meek as a wee lamb.

A loud knocking came from the rear of the storeroom. "Hello? O'Shea?"

Patrick started. In his preoccupation, he'd forgotten about his weekly shipment...and just in time. Now he'd have plenty of whiskey to satisfy a thirsty crowd.

Arch Childers greeted him at the back door with a handshake and smile. "Sorry I'm late. Deliveries took longer than I expected."

Meaning O'Shea's was last on his list of saloons and might not receive anything if he ran out. That didn't sit well. Patrick refused to let the snub put him out of sorts right before Charm showed up. She already thought he had the temperament of a grizzly bear. For her sake, he would remain cheerful. "You're here now, so you're right on time."

Childers returned to his wagon, which he'd parked up next to the building just beyond a barrel of garbage that needed burning. Making deliveries to the rear of the building reduced the chances of being caught selling illegal whiskey. Though with all the other trouble in town, few people paid him any mind. The army had its hands full protecting the railroad tracks, and the sheriff didn't care to enforce a law nobody liked.

The bootlegger tossed a remark over his shoulder. "There's someone out here to see you."

Patrick opened the door wide and stepped outside. Indeed there was…his Charm, sitting on the buckboard seat, wearing the brightest red dress he had ever seen, with her hands folded primly on her lap.

She stared like she'd never seen him before when he went over to assist her. Rather than taking her hand, he grasped her around the waist, lifted her over the mud and set her on the threshold. He didn't know how she'd ended up in the local moonshine distributor's wagon, but he didn't like it. Not one bit.

Biting her head off wouldn't help, and would probably send her running. He forced his lips upward. "Glad to see you're safe. I was beginning to worry."

She kept right on staring at him. "You…you look different."

Different. Not handsome, or good, or even just better. What was her opinion about Childers? Would she say he looked *different*? Patrick's starched collar got tight, his neck hot. He fought to contain his jealousy.

He leaned closer, lowering his voice. "Why did you accept a ride from *him*?"

Her smooth brow furrowed, a puzzled frown. "He was kind enough to offer me one."

Kind, my foot.

Patrick sent Childers a warning look, but he was busy retrieving two large suitcases from the back of the wagon. Charm moved as he set them inside the door. The bulging cases would explode without the heavy straps holding them shut. Looked like she was moving in. The idea didn't distress him, however unlikely. "Those are your costumes? Why didn't you tell me you had so many? I could've gotten them."

Her color deepened. "We'll discuss it later."

"Discuss what?" Her decision to accept a ride? Now he knew why with one look at those heavy suitcases. She wasn't big enough to lift them, much less carry the huge suitcases three blocks. He should've gone after her.

Her gaze shifted over his shoulder and her expression turned to distress. "What in the world...?"

Patrick turned to see what had her so upset. The bootlegger had folded the canvas back, revealing pine coffins. Childers pried the top of one open with a crowbar. He retrieved two ceramic jugs. After setting those by the door, he went back and collected three more.

"What is that?" Charm asked in a hushed voice.

"Liquor." Patrick carried the jugs inside. Later, he would transfer the contents to charred oaken barrels, which would turn the liquor a reddish color and give it a flavor close to bourbon whiskey. Far cheaper than purchasing whiskey from distillers back East and paying ridiculous taxes.

While Charm watched with a look of amazement, he transported the remainder of the jugs into the storeroom. She'd tasted the brandy he made by mixing the brew with fermented fruit—wasn't a lady's drink.

He lifted her heavy cases and set them over by the stairs. Costumes. Couldn't imagine why she needed so many. She would want a place to put them, and to get dressed. He hadn't thought of it earlier and should have. He wasn't doing a very good job taking care of his good luck charm. "You can have one of the rooms upstairs."

Her face paled.

He could've kicked himself. Working women had rooms over saloons. He quickly explained. "A dressing room is what I mean. Nothing else."

"Got everything unloaded…"

Patrick turned at the remark. Childers would have to walk up about the time he stepped on his tongue. "Fine, thanks."

On delivery day, they typically ended up in a long conversation about the finer points of making moonshine or arguing over local politics. Today, Patrick was in no mood to chat. He wanted Childers gone as soon as possible.

The bootlegger gave Charm a flirtatious smile.

Patrick fought the urge to knock the other man's teeth out. "I'll settle with you inside." When he turned to Charm, he softened his tone. "Won't be long. Then I'll take these bags up to your dressing room. The door has a bolt on the inside."

"That's good to know." She looked at him, not Childers.

She followed him into the saloon. Patrick had never been so keenly aware of a woman's presence, and it made him wonder if her magnetism extended to other men. Saints, he hoped not. He might end up killing someone.

He retrieved the lockbox from a drawer in the back bar and counted out what he owed. The cost of homebrew had gone up to twelve dollars a gallon. He'd been forced to raise his prices, but he could still sell drinks for twenty-five cents a shot and make a profit. With Charm performing, he would bring in even more. Enough to pay off his debts and make improvements.

Unless the railroad agent assigned the land to McGill. Then he would lose everything.

He glanced up, caught Charm watching him and gave her a smile. She blushed and looked away. The classic reaction from a woman who found a man attractive.

Maybe her stunned remark earlier meant she liked him looking *different*. She shied away from him when he touched her. That didn't mean she disliked his touch. She might like it too much. And the way she'd fussed over him, not like a mother…more like a wife.

Patrick's heart beat faster. Why was he so bloody slow to see the obvious? She shared this insane attraction, or his name wasn't O'Shea.

He could ask for Charm's hand and his problem would be solved. Marriage to Charm could turn out to be a bigger problem. Desperation made a man risk what he wouldn't otherwise. Knowing the attraction was mutual gave him confidence, and having enough in common to make the marriage sensible made him more comfortable with the idea. Besides, it would benefit both of them. He'd keep his land, and she would have his protection and be kept safe from men who would try to take advantage. She was naïve to think she could bring her things over here and not suffer the consequences. He'd save her from herself.

Patrick handed Childers his money.

The bootlegger folded the bills and tucked them into a leather pouch threaded through a belt that also held a sheath. He adjusted his coat over a bone-handled knife locals called an Arkansas Toothpick. Unlike his brothers, Arch wasn't known for being quarrelsome, yet few were willing to push the strapping young man into a fight. For his part, Patrick avoided confrontations. He'd had enough of killing in the war. However, he'd make an exception if Childers kept sending sheep-eyed looks in Charm's direction.

"Miss LaBelle tells me she's gonna be performing..."

"That's right." Patrick didn't invite Childers to return. Reason told him the more men who came to the show, the more money he'd make. But he'd stopped listening to reason the moment he saw Charm sitting in the bootlegger's wagon.

Childers smoothed his hand over his hair, preening as she watched. "Think I'll come back later so I can see you perform, Miss LaBelle. I bet you sing as pretty as a songbird."

"Thank you, Mr. Childers. I do hope you'll make it back in time to see the show."

Logically, Patrick knew Charm was just being polite. But hearing her issue an invitation to Childers heaped fiery embers on the searing jealousy burning his insides.

Charm belonged to him. The sooner he established that, the better.

"You've got other deliveries to make. I'll see you out the back." Patrick took hold of the younger man's beefy arm.

Childers frowned when he couldn't shake off the grip. "I'm in no hurry."

"Sure you are."

Arch kept his feet planted, the friendly smile fading. The muscles in his arm tensed.

Patrick glanced at the knife. On second thought, a different approach might've been wiser.

"Oh, Mr. O'Shea. I almost forgot. I have a favor to ask." Charm glided over. The moment she laid her hand on his arm, it seemed something inside him unlocked, and his grip on the other man released.

"Excuse me for interrupting..." She acted as if she hadn't noticed they were about to come to blows. Except, her fingers trembled.

"No, ma'am, you ain't interrupting anything. I was on my out." Childers adjusted his coat. With a careless smile, he touched his fingers to the brim of his hat. "Miss LaBelle, it's been my pleasure. Until later."

As soon as the back door slammed shut, Charm turned with an icy glare.

"What is wrong with you?"

Patrick didn't answer right off. Her question could be interpreted a number of ways. She could be referring to his jealousy, or to his stupidity, or to something else entirely.

He made it to the bar without limping and stashed the lockbox in a drawer. His pride had already taken a beating when she stepped in and saved him from having to fight a man who might've whipped him. No, not *might* have. Defeat was a foregone conclusion. Childers had every advantage: health, strength, agility, and a damn big knife.

"You should be careful who you accept rides from..." The moment the rebuke left Patrick's lips, he knew it was the wrong thing to say.

Charm's eyes flashed with fury. "Mr. Childers behaved like a gentleman. You, on the other hand, are being an ass."

She applied the lash with more precision than the officer who'd flayed his bare back, a punishment for being drunk and disorderly. Hadn't he learned anything since then?

More restraint. That's what he needed. Otherwise, he wouldn't be able to stand by calmly while men drooled over his wife, something that was guaranteed to happen as long as she performed. His bad temper had gotten him into trouble too many times to count. He couldn't let it chase off his good luck. That is, if he hadn't already ruined his chance at talking Charm into marrying him.

Charm applauded the restraint she showed by not walking over there and slapping Mr. O'Shea. The impertinent man had some nerve. How dare he rebuke her for accepting a ride when he hadn't bothered to offer his assistance, and then foolishly antagonized the man who came to her aid? He all but challenged Mr. Childers to a fight by trying to drag him out the door.

She shivered, rubbing at the chill on her arms. Had she not intervened, Mr. O'Shea might be sprawled out on the floor with a knife plunged into his chest. It could've happened. She'd seen fights spiral out of control, had witnessed men stabbed to death, shot, struck on the head with a chair, all because they couldn't control their tempers. Or jealousy. That's what appeared to have set him off, though she'd done nothing to provoke it.

Unable to deal with the onslaught of emotions, she turned sharply and set off after her suitcases. Her skirts swirled, throwing bits of caked mud off the hemline, the result of her brief walk with suitcases in tow. Mr. O'Shea had left her bags by the stairs in the rear of the building where liquor and foodstuffs were stored. She would fetch suitcases and take them upstairs herself. She didn't require his assistance.

The storeroom had a distinct odor peculiar to fermented beverages. Canned goods lined the shelves, and on the floor next to casks of beer and whiskey were barrels labeled salt crackers. Greasy sausage links dangled from a nail driven into a beam over her head.

Her stomach growled. Maybe she could have one of those sausage links. She would prefer potpie, except she would choke on it just thinking about those horrid people who put her out in the street.

Mr. O'Shea caught up and reached the suitcases before she did. He moved fast, given his limp. His legs were so much longer than hers, he made the distance in half the time.

"Miss LaBelle…Charm…" He stammered her name.

She hadn't seen him so awkward. Embarrassed, perhaps. He ought to be.

"You ran off before I…" His eyes begged forgiveness. "Here, let me get these suitcases. I'll show you to your dressing room, and get you something to eat. Don't want you thinking I starve all my workers."

The dimpled smile melted her heart. She restrained her fear, which told her to throw herself into his arms and beg him to promise her to never get into a fight, to never leave her.

She stared at him, horrified, as a different kind of fear took hold. The devilish man had infected her…with sentimentalism. Something she never suffered from before. Dramatic emotions were reserved for the stage, not real life.

"After you." He nodded at the stairs leading into the unknown.

Her hand trembled and she grasped the railing. The risers behind her creaked and groaned. He followed at an uneven pace. She grew worried. "Are the suitcases too heavy?

"No…though you weigh less." Teasing, his way of rebuffing her concern, or deflecting attention away from his infirmity. She didn't really think of him as infirm. He towered over her, and he looked very strong. Whatever caused his limp didn't get in his way.

She found his light-heartedness refreshing and his tenacity admirable. Jealousy, she wouldn't stand for. He didn't own her. No one would.

When she reached the top of the stairs, she hesitated. Afternoon light filtered in through a window at the end of the hall, reflecting off bare walls. Unmarked doors faced each other.

Mr. O'Shea stepped behind her. His nearness triggered an invisible current that leapt between them. The sensation wasn't unpleasant or frightening. Just odd. She'd never experienced anything like it.

"The room on the left. You can have that one for your dressing room."

She gave the knob a twist and pushed the door. A warm breeze flowing between two open windows ruffled curls around her face. The room had simple furnishings: a bed covered by a wool blanket that was folded back over what looked like clean sheets, a washstand with a utilitarian basin and pitcher, and beneath, a chamber pot. Beside the bed stood a small table, and next to that, a straight-back chair. Instead of a wardrobe, a row of pegs were nailed into a board mounted near the door. Nothing fancy, but it afforded more privacy than what she had at the hotel.

She swallowed to relieve a dry mouth, working up the nerve to ask if he would allow her to stay. Living above a saloon would virtually guarantee she'd be considered a prostitute. What choice did she have? At this point, her reputation was irreparably tarnished.

He carried her suitcases inside. "Where do you want them?"

She stared at the bed, trembling. He might assume she wanted to use the room to entertain customers—him being one of them. Her throat tightened and her eyes began to sting. She swallowed, dangerously close to breaking down.

In hindsight, she might've stayed with the other women and tried to negotiate with the railroad agent for more time. That would only delay the inevitable. She'd made her decision. Now she had to live with it.

Mr. O'Shea set one suitcase on the chair and put the other one on the bed, which creaked beneath the weight. He glanced at her with amusement dancing in his eyes. "How many costumes do you have in here?"

"That one isn't my costumes. It's my clothes, all my things…"

He frowned, clearly confused.

She took a deep breath. "The owners of the hotel asked me to leave."

There, that wasn't so hard.

Her employer advanced with a thunderous frown. "Are you sayin' they threw you out because I hired you?"

"No. Because I took the job." She refused to let him shoulder any of the blame.

His fierce frown softened, followed by a look of respect, and then, tenderness, a surprising response. "Hypocrites, the lot of 'em. You got no cause for shame."

"I know." The tension banding her chest eased. Sharing her pain with him made the load lighter, less oppressive. Knowing he understood and sympathized made it easier to ask for a favor. "If you don't mind, I'd like to rent a room. I need somewhere to stay."

"I'll do better than that."

Charm pondered what he meant by the cryptic remark, but then her thoughts scattered when he lifted his hand to her face. Every muscle coiled in anticipation of the dreaded, gut-wrenching response. Instead, a warm and comforting feeling invaded her body. She couldn't make sense of her reaction, hadn't thought she could experience desire without fear.

"You'll be safe with me, I promise."

Patrick O'Shea was only man besides her father she'd trusted to catch her, despite knowing where blind dependence could lead. She shouldn't rely on him, but all the reasons in the world didn't seem to matter. Somehow, she found her hands on his arms, clinging to him.

"Don't cry," he murmured.

"I'm not crying."

"Your cheeks are wet."

Even tears were a surprise. Frozen emotions, melting.

He moved his thumb over her skin, the light friction sending shivers racing in every direction. His touch triggered a yearning so strong she leaned forward, tempted to give him permission to do more than cup her cheek.

The ache spread and became urgent, compelling. She teetered on the edge of desperation, and only he had the keys to a storeroom filled with secret pleasures. She rubbed her face against his palm, nudging him to do something, to ease the restless hunger.

His breath blew warm against her skin an instant before his mouth touched hers.

He didn't force her lips apart, or grind his teeth against the tender flesh, as she anticipated. He cradled her head with his hands, moving his fingers in soothing circles on her scalp as he brushed feather-light kisses over her mouth, leaving her lips tingling and her body aching. With her senses fully engaged, her mind was too busy to dwell on fear.

Gradually, he increased the lush pressure until it felt so good the ache became impossible to ignore. She tilted her head at his tender lead, letting him coax her into deepening the kiss. That felt better, though it didn't relieve the ache. Not entirely. If she could get closer perhaps that would help.

Wrapping her arms around his neck, she threaded her

fingers through his hair. Soft, like her favorite cashmere shawl. She drowned in a sensual flood of taste and texture, swaying against him, her desire increasing as he worked magic with his mouth and fingers. Trailing kisses down her neck, he caressed her shoulders, arms and back, touching her with a kind of careful reverence reserved for fragile objects.

Overcome by his gentle invasion, her defenses crumbled. Strangely enough, she didn't care because she didn't want to keep him out, her unlikely knight. With resolute tenderness, he cut away the thorns surrounding her heart. Hurtful memories gave way to something stronger than fear and more powerful than despair. Whatever this feeling, it was exquisite, like nothing she'd ever experienced.

His hand slid up the side of her ribcage and he shaped the underside of her breast, held up by the corset. Her nipples stiffened, her skin grew warm, her chest compressed. The tightness could be on account of the special corset, which she wore to give the illusion of fuller breasts. She half expected him to point out the deception. Again, he surprised her, touching her like she'd offered him something rare and precious.

She trembled with apprehension, excitement, and, astonishingly, eagerness.

His questing fingers drew the scooping neckline lower.

Surprise jolted through her. Strong enough to startle her out of the seductive stupor. With a gasp, she jerked away. Her hand flew to her lips, still damp and swollen from his kisses.

How had this happened? She hardly knew the man, yet she'd been eager to give herself to him, had behaved like a harlot. That must be what he assumed when he encountered no resistance. Even knowing better, she still longed for his touch.

Shame flooded her face. She caught a sharp breath on a sob.

He shook his head like he was trying to clear it. When he reached for her, she backed away, another whimper escaping. His expression changed from dazed to remorse. He dropped his hand. "*Stóirín*, don't be fearing me. I'd ne'r harm a hair on yer head. I only want to take care of you, protect you...if you'll let me."

His brogue thickened and he called her by a name she didn't understand. Who was this man she'd let kiss and fondle her? Her father had scorned the Irish for their uneven temperament. Her mother had dubbed them slothful. Patrick didn't fit the image of the drunken, lazy Finn depicted by apish caricatures in the newspapers. But what did she know about him, really? She knew nothing, other than the fact that she'd fallen victim to his seduction.

Simon had ruined her. This Irish charmer had the power to turn her into a whore.

Confusion rattled her wits.

"Please...please leave...." Her plea came out in a high, wavering voice she didn't recognize. She dredged up courage and managed to address him in a calm, remote tone. "I need to get ready for the show tonight. If you'd be so kind as to leave so I can have some privacy."

He hesitated, and then heaved a sigh. "All right, I'll go. We haven't got time for a long discussion now anyway. But later, we'll be having a talk."

Her fear spiked. The very idea! Having a conversation about her inexcusable lapse of judgment. He had to be mad.

She moved another step away. "There's nothing to talk about."

His features hardened in a look of pure determination. "Yes, there is. I mean to marry you, Charm."

Chapter Six

Laughter echoed off the walls of the saloon as Charm strutted across the stage in an oversized frock coat. "Come now, gentlemen. Take a good look at these fine ladies...." She whipped off a silk top hat with a sign tucked into the band that read *Official Matchmaker*, and motioned to twelve male volunteers who'd joined her on the stage, dressed in wigs and lacy shawls. Tablecloths had become skirts.

One of the "brides" pointed the toe of his boot and twisted his hips while fluttering his eyelashes. The audience responded with hoots and catcalls. Charm smacked his arm and waved her finger in his face, scolding him for flirting.

Patrick remained on guard from his position at the edge of the stage, keeping an eye on the rowdy crowd, at the same time trying to watch the hilarious performance. He'd hired a bartender and two working girls to take care of serving customers so he could focus on protecting Charm, not trusting anyone else with her safety.

Her antics had the crowd mesmerized. No one would

guess she'd been so upset earlier she had stayed locked in her dressing room until time for her debut. He had managed to get her to take a bowl of stew, but she wouldn't let him in. Fine. He would wait until after the show to secure her agreement to marry him.

She took long swinging strides across the stage, aping the railroad agent's mannerisms right down to the unfriendly glower. Spinning around, she projected her voice over the laughter. "You won't find women like these anywhere in the territory…"

That was a sure bet, she couldn't have selected a homelier bunch.

"As agent for the railroad, I have the responsibility of seeing these ladies married off tonight. They can cook, sew, plant a garden, dig a well…" She counted each trait on her fingers. "And plow your fields!"

Howling laughter erupted.

"I'll plow your field," hollered an inebriated settler near the front.

Patrick tightened his grip on the baseball bat in case any of the men got too excited. With a bat, he could take down three attackers in less time than it took to cock the hammer on a revolver after dispatching one bullet. He wouldn't kill his customers, just crack a few heads.

Charm didn't act like she'd heard the coarse remark. She caught one of the volunteers by the arm and pulled him to the front of the stage. "I hear this lovely lass can skin buffalo!"

Bob Scritchfield, better known as Buffalo Bob, grinned, displaying a mouthful of tobacco-stained teeth. His wig sat askew and golden curls dangled over a thick black beard covering most of his face. "Skin yer own dang buffalo," he bellowed.

She raised her hands high. "Do any of you fine gentlemen want one of our brides?"

"Yes!" the men in the audience roared.

Charm whipped up the crowd better than a traveling evangelist peddling salvation.

"Well, boys, here's all you gotta do." Settling the hat on her head, she marched over to a small chest on a table at the side of the stage and gathered a handful of newspaper clippings cut to resemble greenbacks. "Pay the railroad LOTS of money!"

Laughter turned to loud booing.

Patrick watched, amused. She pranced over to where he stood and lifted the bundle high. Fake money rained down on him. "Mr. O'Shea doesn't want one of our brides. He wants a performer to bring him riches."

Cheeky monkey. She rubbed his nose in his own words...more or less. He'd never said anything about riches, and had made it perfectly clear how much he wanted to marry her. Something he intended to settle later tonight.

"Do I get my pick?" yelled a man at the back of the crowd.

"I'll take the railroad agent!" Arch Childers waved at Charm. The bootlegger must not value his skin.

Patrick tapped the bat against his palm in warning. He didn't experience the mad rush of jealousy because now he knew Charm had a weakness for him. Her prancing and posturing on stage was an act. The way she responded to his kiss, that wasn't an act. Although it appeared to surprise her, based on how flustered she got—right before she threw him out of her room.

He wouldn't regret kissing her, but he should've waited until after the performance and proposed to her first. Discovering their mutual attraction had given him the courage he needed to ask for her hand. Well, he hadn't asked, exactly. He'd informed her that he intended to marry her. After the show, he would ask properly. They could be wed before the next night's performance and he would make an announcement. That would put an end to any ideas these horny settlers had, including Arch Childers.

After the bride lottery skit, Charm ducked behind a canvas curtain hung across the back of the stage. When she reemerged, she'd shed the coat and hat. She sat on a chair, arranged the skirt of her pretty red grown, strummed her banjo and began to sing.

The room quieted down at the mournful ballad. The lyrics were silly, something about a sailor and a mermaid, but she sang it with such heartfelt emotion he got choked up.

McLaughlin lurched out of his seat and staggered toward the stage. "M'god, she's fizzing!"

Patrick planted his hand on front of the man's shoulder. "She's brilliant, I agree. Now take your seat. No one's allowed near the stage."

"But I can't see her from over there." McLaughlin blinked, bleary-eyed.

"You won't see any better from up here."

"Tell ya what, I'll protect her and you go sit down." McLaughlin draped his arm around Patrick's shoulders and leaned in, whispering loudly. "Gonna ask her to marry me."

The man stank to high heaven. Only a sow would accept his suit.

"She's already spoken for..." Patrick unwound McLaughlin's arm and pushed him away.

"Who's the lucky fellow?"

"Me."

McLaughlin's eyes got big. Then a laugh burst out of him. "Oh, I get it. That's a joke..."

"It's not a joke." Patrick raised the bat.

The obnoxious drunk held up his hands, still laughing, and reeled away in the direction of his seat.

Patrick noticed none of the other men paid the disturbance any mind, being too engrossed in Charm's performance. Good thing he hadn't put up those ropes. If Charm had been swinging overhead, tempting these coyotes with her lacy petticoats and pretty ankles, he would've gone into a foam-mouthed fit and killed every man in the room.

The banjo twanged. Her voice lifted over the shouts from the crowd as she launched into *An Irish Volunteer*. She'd leapt into his arms the last time she sang it. He wouldn't mind it if she did that again.

She marched in place, her multicolored petticoats flashing from beneath the hem of her skirt. The red silk dress gleamed in the light of two-dozen candles lining the front of the stage. When he could afford it, he'd bathe her in limelight. She glowed with exuberance, even brighter than the lights. This brightness came from inside, and she projected it into the far corners of the room, banishing the darkness. So beautiful and talented, and to think, she would soon be his wife.

He willed her to look at him so he could offer her a proud smile.

Her gaze dropped and their eyes met. She stepped out of beat...paused, her face reddening...and then went right back to strumming her banjo, establishing the rhythm once more. No one appeared to notice. They went right on shouting and singing along.

Patrick returned his attention to the rowdy crowd. He resisted the temptation to smile—not because she'd stumbled, he felt bad about that—because he was the only man in the room who was able to rattle her. Her flustered reaction he took as a good sign.

After the show came to an end, he herded the crowd out the door, including men who had to be assisted or carried away. He paid the bartender and the two working girls he'd hired to help serve drinks. If the whores plied their trade afterwards, it was none of his business. But they weren't allowed to entertain customers upstairs, especially now that Charm lived here.

She had exited through the crowd, throwing kisses, bidding the men *adieu*, and disappeared through the rear door on her way up to her dressing room.

Patrick's anticipation had reached a fever pitch by the time he placed the bar over the front door and followed her upstairs with a bottle and two glasses in his hands. He'd managed to obtain a bottle of French Cognac and wanted to offer her a congratulatory drink before he went down on one knee.

He knocked on her door, and waited.

"Charm?" He knocked again.

She might be in bed. She'd been through a lot. Evicted and kissed, all in the same day. Ironic, how things turned out for the best. She'd come to him with her defenses down, needing him. He would take good care of her.

He twisted the knob. The door wouldn't budge. Had she bolted it to keep others out—or just him? Growing uneasy, he knocked harder. "Are you awake? I've got a surprise…a nice one. Something you'll like."

She had to be dead to the world, or she wanted him to think so.

Patrick put his ear to the door. Only gossipy biddies snooped at doors, but he'd already done things he never thought he would do where Charm was concerned. Asking her to marry him, for one. He couldn't hear anything. Not even the sound of breathing by the door.

She had to be sleeping, not ignoring him.

He straightened and released a disappointed sigh. He could understand why she'd collapse after that exhausting performance, it wasn't the thought of marrying him that sent her running. At least, that's what he'd keep telling himself until he saw her again in the morning.

Daylight flooded the room when Charm finally crawled out of bed. She threw the sheets and blanket over the petticoats she'd stripped off the night before. Her dresses and undergarments were strewn about the room. She sighed, too tired to pick them up.

Fatigue had pulled her into a deep sleep shortly before dawn. Long after Mr. O'Shea had given up on having their "talk." After demonstrating he could easily seduce her, he'd calmly informed her he intended to marry her only a few hours before she had to go onstage. By some miracle, she'd gathered her scattered wits and performed. Only stumbling once, when she caught the devilish charmer watching her with a possessive look in his eyes.

He enjoyed keeping her off balance. She would be prepared for him today.

She cleaned up as best she could with a pitcher of water, a cake of strong soap and a threadbare towel—a far cry from the scented baths she was used to taking. Combing the tangles out of her hair took longer. She would deal with dressing it after she found something to eat.

A knock at the door made her jump. She'd barely gotten out of bed, and he was back again? Last night she'd ignored him. He wouldn't go away again, and at some point she had to face him, get control of the situation and manage his expectations. Neither task would be easy. He'd demonstrated how stubborn he could be...and how persuasive.

"Yes?"

"Good, you're up. Are you hungry?"

Her stomach had collapsed in on itself. "I could eat something."

"I've made you breakfast."

He cooked? Well, of course he did. He had to eat. But to make her a meal as well, that showed he was thoughtful, as well as self-sufficient.

"Food sounds wonderful. Give me a moment..."

If he'd brought her a plate, she could eat in her room, which meant she didn't have to talk to him...much. She grabbed a blue cotton day dress from a wad of clothes in the suitcase and pulled it over her head, buttoning the front. Padding barefooted to the door, she opened it a crack.

Her employer greeted her with a smile. Was he always this cheerful in the morning? "Good, you're still here. I was beginning to think you'd slipped out the window."

If he'd provided the ropes she asked for, she might have. "Not before breakfast."

His smile deepened, revealing twin dimples.

Charm swallowed her heart before it leapt out of her throat. Yesterday, she'd been shocked at seeing him clean-shaven and dressed like a gentleman. She admired the lines of his strong jaw. His beautiful light eyes were more noticeable, and that devastating smile. She could suggest he grow the beard again. That way, she wouldn't be tempted to stare at him, which she was doing right now.

Her grumbling stomach broke the trance.

A frown creased his brow. "You need to eat."

"I thought you said you brought me breakfast."

"No, I said I *made* you breakfast." He gestured to the door across the hall.

Charm trembled. The shivers running up and down her arms had nothing to do with being cold. The air was quite warm. "You want me to…join you…in your bedroom?"

His eyes crinkled with amusement. "Might be better if I served you in the kitchen. I've got your breakfast in there."

In order to eat, she had to enter the lion's den. Demanding he deliver breakfast to her room would be rude, and he'd already gone beyond any expectation she should have. She had managed to ward off overenthusiastic suitors for years. Granted, she had help: a protective father and a zealous mother, and later, her manager, although Simon only saved her so he could have her for himself. Mr. O'Shea hadn't forced his attentions on her, but he seemed to think he should make her respectable and wed her. Today, she would set him straight.

Charm ventured across the hall into what appeared to be a combination sitting room and kitchen. All very cozy, and surprisingly neat, considering he lived alone and men were known to be messy creatures. Virtuous women were neat and orderly. Another strike against her.

Her eyes darted to an open doorway leading to another room. His bedroom? She squelched her curiosity and jerked her attention to the table in the kitchen area. Eat, and then leave as quickly as possible. The less time spent in his private quarters, the better.

She passed a large framed mirror mounted on the wall. That was a mistake. Seeing her washed-out reflection only reminded her how bad she looked in the morning. Turning away from her reflection, she tossed loose hair over her shoulder, would've preferred pulling it in front of her face. Oh, what did it matter anyway? If he saw her at her worst, he would change his mind quick enough about wanting to marry her.

"If you'd like, I'll put that mirror in your room. None

of my other guests needed one for anything besides shaving."

"That explains why the one in there is only large enough to see my mouth."

He maintained a disgustingly jovial mood as he pulled out her chair. On the blue-and-white checkered tablecloth, a single place had been set with a fork and knife and a folded napkin. Evidence that he had expected her to capitulate.

What else did he expect?

Growing nervous, she rearranged her skirt, checked the tortoiseshell buttons down the front of her dress. This feeling of being exposed had to come from not wearing her corset and padding and layers of petticoats. Without them, she resembled an underfed waif. "I'm not really dressed for dining out."

When she started to stand, he gripped her shoulders and held her in place. "You aren't dining out. Now sit still and stop fidgeting."

After fetching a coffeepot from atop the stove, he poured the steaming brew into two ceramic cups. She lifted the coffee to her nose, inhaling gratefully before taking a sip.

"Mmm. You make good coffee."

"Here's something I can't take credit for making." He moved a wire basket to the table and removed a napkin, revealing a loaf of sliced bread, and nestled next to it, a tub of butter. "Mrs. Appleton's brown bread."

Charm slathered butter on a slice, remembering her manners about the time she took a bite. "Thank you," she mumbled around a mouthful.

"More on the way." He went back to the oven and used a kitchen cloth to withdraw a plate of food. Keeping it warm for her. How sweet.

"Should've fed you better yesterday." He set the plate in front of her. "Meat pie, with potatoes and onions."

"Oh, it smells delicious. Is this from Mrs. Appleton, too?"

"No. That, I made."

She took a bite. The flaky crust and savory filling tasted even better than Mrs. Fry's potpie. "You've mastered coffee and cooking. I'm impressed."

He took the chair across the table and picked up his cup, regarded her with a pleased smile. "*A handful of skill is better than a bagful of gold*, as they say."

"Another old folks' proverb?"

"That one's from me sainted mother, and never let it be said I called her old." He leaned back and took a sip of coffee.

Charm paused with her fork in hand. "Your family is from Ireland, I presume?"

"Was it the accent that gave me away, or the proverb?"

"The proverb, of course." She went back to eating, more slowly, being somewhat sated and enjoying their conversation. She wanted to know more about him and his *sainted mother*, and *the old folks*, as he called them, what his family had been like and whether he had siblings. As an only child, she'd longed for a brother or sister. But if she probed, it would invite his questions, and she wasn't ready to open that door.

"Where is your food? Aren't you eating?"

"I ate hours ago."

"Hours? What time is it?"

He pulled a watch from his vest pocket. "Close to noon."

"Oh..." She took the napkin from her lap and wiped her mouth. He must consider her a slug. "I tend to sleep late after performances."

"Can't imagine why, what with all that singing and dancing." He nodded at her half-finished meal. "You need to eat more. You're so tiny you'll blow away."

People often assumed her small size implied weakness. "I'm stronger than I look."

He set his cup down. The tenderness that came over his face made her heart quiver. "Even a strong woman needs someone to take care of her. Marry me Charm."

So that was his plan. Bring her in here and feed her to demonstrate how well he could take care of her so she would accept his proposal. She couldn't fault his consideration, and he was surprisingly sweet when he shed the gruff exterior. Still, his motive for marrying her couldn't be anything more than pure selfishness. Exerting control, that's how men cared for women. There was no reason to think Mr. O'Shea would be any different—even if she wanted him to be.

Tiny waves disturbed the coffee's black surface. Her trembling hands were the blame. She set down her cup. Now, she had to put an end to her fantasies about him, as well as any expectations he might have where she was concerned. "Mr. O'Shea, I am quite capable of taking care of myself. In fact, I prefer it."

His eyes gleamed with amusement. "Patrick."

"What?"

"We know each other well enough, you can call me Patrick."

"Did you hear what I said?"

Still smiling, he leaned back and folded his arms over his chest in a way that suggested supreme confidence. "You said you prefer to take care of yourself. If you want to do the cooking, I won't argue."

He wasn't stupid, so she could only assume he wasn't taking her seriously.

"You know I'm not talking about cooking."

"Then what are you talking about?"

Her temper flared. "Let me clarify. I don't need *you* to take care of me."

The moment his smile faded, her conscience pricked.

Regardless of his motivation, he had been thoughtful, kinder than she deserved.

"What I mean to say is, I'm very grateful for all you've done, for cooking me breakfast, and for letting me have a room, and for the job..."

"Don't forget the stage."

"Oh, yes. And for building the stage..." She tried to think of anything else she might've missed. The best kiss she ever had, but she wasn't thanking him for that.

"You're welcome." He stood and gathered the dishes, took them over to a dry sink, where he stacked them. "I'll wash these later." He glanced around with an arched eyebrow. "Unless you'd rather do it?"

Why was she sitting here letting him wait on her? It just proved his point, that she needed someone because she wasn't capable of doing for herself. She jerked up out of the chair and pushed him out of the way. "I'll clean up."

"Don't bother with those. I'm just teasing..." He caught her by the arm and hauled her up against him, bent down and began to nuzzle her hair and kiss her cheek. "We have better things to do than wash dishes."

His playful affection startled her. But her instinctive response, putting her arms around him, shook her to her core. Panicked, she pushed him away. "Get your hands off me!"

"They're off..." He held his hands up in the air. "Don't get upset. I just wanted to give you a wee kiss."

Not for a second did she believe he would stop at a *wee kiss*. She backed away, bumped into the chair and had to catch it to prevent it from falling. Never was she clumsy. The reason had to be this frightening vulnerability he stirred up whenever he came near.

She trembled, fought fear with anger. "What makes you think I welcome your attentions? I don't want you to kiss me! I want to be left alone."

The dense man didn't even look offended. He frowned as if puzzled by her reaction. "What's wrong, *stóirín?*"

So many things were wrong, not the least of which was her unwanted attraction to a man she hardly knew and wasn't sure she could trust. "Don't call me that."

"It just means *wee darling.*"

He wooed her using sweet words and tender gestures. With one kiss, he could dissolve her restraint. He wouldn't need to use force to bend her to his will.

She hugged her arms to keep from running into his. "I've made my position clear, Mr. O'Shea. I'm not interested in being your *wee darling*, or anything other than your employee. If you can't respect my decision, I'll seek a job elsewhere."

Chapter Seven

The following Saturday, Patrick's hopes hit rock bottom before noon. He'd failed to convince Gilly's brother to release his claim on the property. Even offering McGill a portion of the profits hadn't worked. The scurvy dog said he'd just pay off what was owed on the loan, so the saloon would be his, too, and all the profit. To cap the climax, the railroad agent had a *Closed* sign on his door.

Patrick used his hands to block the light and peered through the window of the darkened land office. Hardt had been gone for several days. Didn't matter. Patrick knew he would get the same response he'd gotten the last time he'd come by to plead his case.

"Come back when you're married."

Easier said than done. Not only had Charm rebuffed him, she seemed intent on ignoring him completely, except for when she wanted her take each night. She played to packed crowds, and she was right, he made more on drinks than he had ever made. He still didn't have enough to pay off the building, or McGill, greedy bastard. Soon, Hardt's decision would be made and it would be too late.

He had to convince Charm to marry him.

Patrick headed back to the saloon in time to open for lunch. He adjusted a hatbox under his arm. On a spur of the moment, he had stopped into the dry goods store to find a gift for her. Mr. Middaugh had suggested a new bonnet. Patrick hoped Charm liked the one he picked out. Might have too many flowers. He knew nothing about buying for women. Kathleen had dropped obvious hints about what she wanted. Charm never asked for anything.

A thunder of hooves caught his attention.

Wagons pulled over to make way for the cavalry patrol. Their mounts kicked up dirt and dust as they rode south, likely headed for the railroad construction route.

Outside the saloon, McLaughlin and three of his friends leaned against the wall, following the soldiers with narrowed eyes.

The army had managed to maintain a semblance of peace after putting down the riots that had reached their peak earlier in the year. But the vandalism continued, and three counties remained under martial law. Other than occasional harassment, the army hadn't taken direct action against leaders of the militant Land League. But if the soldiers noticed four members of the organization hanging around the saloon, they might suspect something was going on.

On the other hand, McLaughlin and his friends weren't doing anything wrong and they were customers. "Here for food or drink?" Patrick asked the men, as he unlocked the door.

He would fight for his rights, whether against McGill, the railroad or the U.S. Army. Battles, he understood. Women, not so much.

The four men filed in behind him. The last one shut the door.

Patrick turned, surprised. "What are you doing? I'm opening up."

McLaughlin hooked his straw hat on a set of antlers. "We need a place to meet. You're a member of the league. We figured you wouldn't mind us using the saloon for a little while. We'll pay for our drinks."

The request, if it could be called that, came at a bad time, and Patrick wasn't in the mood to pretend friendliness. "You bet you'll pay, but no meeting. Not here."

If Hardt found out, he'd sign the land over to McGill without batting an eye. The railroad had announced they would not do business with anyone who aided the Land League; and the army had orders to bust up meetings—or bust heads.

Patrick set the hatbox beneath the bar. He wanted to take the gift up to Charm, except he had to tend bar until his part-time help showed up. Later, before her performance, he would have a chance to see her. He hoped the hat pleased her enough to give him another chance. He couldn't push her, at the same time, he had to hurry up and get married before he lost the saloon. Ruminating over the dilemma, he shrugged off his coat and hung it on a hook next to the shelves.

"Boys, get a table, I'll join you in a minute." McLaughlin stepped up to the bar. "Pour a round of drinks and come join us. I think you'll be interested in hearing what we got planned."

Patrick glared. "Have you lost your hearing? I said you can't meet here."

McLaughlin pulled a cigar from inside his coat, which confirmed he was deaf...or begging to be tossed out on his duff. He continued to unload items from his pockets, including a watch, a deck of cards and a handful of change.

He patted his coat as if searching for something else, and then heaved a sigh. "Just my luck…no matches."

Patrick fished out a block of matches and set them on the bar. "Keep it. Just take your meetings elsewhere."

McLaughlin broke off a match, puffing as he lit his cigar. "I don't understand. I thought you were on our side."

That pretty well summed up the problem. Men picked sides instead of resolving disputes. This country had fought a civil war because of that kind of thinking. Patrick was sick of it.

"There's a good chance I could lose my saloon. It's a given if you're caught meeting here. Does that explain it well enough?"

McLaughlin took a moment to consider the remark. He removed the cigar from his lips, and smoke wreathed his face. "We're your friends, Patrick. If you need our help, all you have to do is ask for it."

Tempting, the thought of asking the Land League to persuade McGill to leave town. Then the favor would have to be returned, and things would go downhill from there. No. Fighting McGill would have to be a personal battle.

"There's nothing you can do." Patrick lined up four glasses and poured drinks. "Except not hold a meeting here. Have a drink, and then be on your way."

McLaughlin scooped up the items on the bar and returned them to his pockets, except for the deck of cards. He pushed it toward Patrick. "Here, I just bought those at the mercantile. Take them, in exchange for the matches. There's some nice pictures on the cards."

Patrick turned the box over in his hand. On the back was a photograph. A pretty woman looked over her bare shoulder, smiling suggestively. "You're giving me naughty pictures for matches?"

McLaughlin laughed. "I kept the ones with the best pictures. Those have photographs of actresses. I'll show you." He took the box and pried open the top, pulled out a card. "This one says its Adah Menken. There's a picture of her tied to a horse..." Bill squinted at the image. "Looks like she's naked." He glanced up at Patrick, and grinned. "Guess I didn't keep all the good ones."

He handed Patrick the box, then gathered his drinks and returned to the table.

"Don't let me catch you talkin' politics," Patrick warned him.

"We'll look at the other pictures." McLaughlin called over his shoulder.

Good, that ought to keep them out of trouble.

Patrick spilled the cards into his hand, his curiosity piqued. He thumbed through the deck until one image stopped him. The young actress looked like Charm right down to her golden ringlets. A filmy white dress billowed around her as if a strong wind blew. The fact that she seemed unaware of the way the thin fabric hugged her form made the image more provocative. His body reacted to the sensual imagery while his mind balked at accepting what was right before his eyes.

He read the name below the photograph in swirling cursive.

Juliette DuCharme, La Belle Enfant.

He didn't know this woman, but he had fantasies about one who looked like her.

Charm LaBelle.

The truth landed a sharp blow to his heart. The conniving little actress had deceived him. Even after he'd made a fool of himself by asking her to marry him. Not once, but twice.

He rubbed his thumb over the image. The ache in his chest worsened. All the warnings had been there.

Ignored. He chose to believe she wanted him because he wanted her.

Another unlucky break. Or maybe none of his failures had a damn thing to do with luck, only making wrong assumptions. Walking into things blindly. Letting his heart rule instead of his head. Like when he set out for America, expecting a land where gold lined the streets just waiting to be picked up. Or signing up with the army, thinking he'd just march around, get paid and eat good food. Asking a spoiled, selfish girl to marry him without anticipating the inevitable mutiny. He set his sights higher this time, and hadn't even realized it.

No, that wasn't true. He knew. Had known from the moment he met Charm that she was unique. In spite of his past failures and every sign that the future would bring more of the same, he still reached for the glittering treasure.

The hatbox under the bar mocked him. Charm wouldn't need a new bonnet. She'd have dozens, along with her pick of men. No wonder she reacted the way she did when he'd proposed. Famous actresses didn't wed lame saloon owners with nothing to offer.

Famous actresses also didn't show up in his saloon, looking for a job.

Patrick frowned at the card, puzzling the mystery. Why would she change her name and sign up for the bride train? Not to find a husband, she'd made that clear enough. She had to be on the run. What better place to run than to a settlement on the edge of the wilderness where few would expect her or recognize her.

She hadn't worn that white dress. If she had, he would've locked her in her room. An appealing idea, if he could get away with it.

He slipped the card into his pocket, and fished out a small flask he kept with him when he went out, in case he needed something to numb the pain. Taking a swig, he hardly noticed how bitter it tasted. Nor did he care. He wouldn't take so much he couldn't think straight. God knows he needed clear thinking for a change. No more dreams about pots of gold or improbable matches made by luck or God or saints. He had one goal, to secure his land and his livelihood…and Charm was going to help him.

Charm buried her head under the covers at the second round of knocking, harder than the first. Did Patrick never sleep? He retired late, got up early. Something had to be wrong with him that he could make do with so little rest.

Knock, knock, knock.

"Oh, all right! I'm coming." She flung the covers off, bleary-eyed, and stumbled over to the suitcase, digging for her wrapper. A week's reprieve he'd given her, and during that time he hadn't bothered her. That was what she wanted, to be left alone. She shouldn't have been miserable about it.

Today she would get out for a few hours and clear her mind. Since being evicted, she hadn't gone anywhere for fear she would be ridiculed. She would have to face her former friends at some point, and it would be best to get it over with. In the meantime, she would find out why Patrick had come knocking, and tell him to leave her be.

She opened the door a crack, enough to peer out, but not so much that he could see more than a sliver of her face. She, on the other hand, could see him just fine. He had on a nice suit, looked very handsome, except for the scowl. "What is it?"

"We need to have a private conversation."

Sometimes his humor could be hard to decipher, but this...this was just downright funny. He couldn't really think she would open the door. "Is that so? Pray tell, why?"

"A personal matter. Believe me, you don't want anyone else to overhear. Let me in, or you come over to my room. Either way, it doesn't matter."

He was serious...no, he was mad, and now, he'd made her angry.

"I am trying to get some rest, so I would appreciate it if you would cease knocking. Whatever it is we need to discuss, we can do it later. Downstairs."

She shut the door, firmly.

"Fine," he called out. "When you come downstairs, I'll introduce everyone to Juliette DuCharme..." His voice faded and the sound of his steps receded.

Charm's heart ceased beating, or so it seemed. God help her. He'd discovered the truth, and planned to tell everyone. Her secret would be out.

She would leave. Except, she didn't have enough money to get very far.

What could she do? Stop him.

She jerked into action, flinging the door open. "Wait!"

Patrick stood a few feet away with his arms crossed over his chest, wearing a smug smile. *Curse him.* He'd tricked her into opening the door.

She looked out into the hallway, both directions. No one else around. She grabbed his arm, dragged him inside her room and slammed the door. Then she whirled around, fists clenched at her sides, frightened, also furious because he meant to scare her by revealing he knew her identity. It might only be a guess. He had no proof.

"What are you talking about?"

Patrick reached inside his coat, withdrew a card, a queen, and held it up, sandwiched between two fingers.

When he turned his hand, a photographic image appeared.

She caught a sharp breath. Oh God. Now she remembered. Simon had paid a man to take pictures of her in that white dress. He'd apparently sold her image to be put on playing cards and didn't tell her, and she would never see a penny of whatever he negotiated. How many of those cards existed? She couldn't escape her past if her picture kept turning up.

"A very good likeness, don't you think?" Patrick's lips twisted into a smile that wasn't warm or kind.

Charm considered grabbing the card and tearing it into pieces. That wouldn't help. There were more wherever that one came from. He had her at his mercy, and he knew it.

He turned the card, looked at it and then frowned at her. His disapproval landed like a fist to the soft part of her belly.

"Patrick, please…" She put her hand over her mouth to stop the miserable plea. Begging wouldn't help. Gone was the gentle giant, and in his place stood a cold stranger. Even his eyes looked different. The dark centers eclipsed all but a thin ring of blue, making them appear empty. She ached to see the familiar tenderness that warmed her like a low fire. The only fires she might see in that impenetrable gaze would be blazing anger.

Unable to bear it, she turned away. She would put up with his passionate kisses and affectionate teasing, if only he would forgive for deceiving him. How he must hate her.

Foreboding prickled her skin. The fact that he came up here before he exposed her falsehood could mean he planned to blackmail her. She had nothing except her meager earnings. He might take the money, and then where would she be? Stuck out here, unable to get away. The idea wouldn't be so repellent if she were stuck with the other Patrick.

She hugged her wrapper, shivering. "What…what do you want?"

"First, tell me why you're here."

No point lying about it. He had found her out, so she would be better off telling him the truth and appealing to his decency.

"That might take awhile." She picked up two dresses flung over the back of the chair and tossed them across her bed, then gestured for him to take a seat.

When she sank onto the bed, Patrick moved one of the dresses aside and sat next to her. His weight pressed down the mattress and she slid against him. His warmth seeped through her wrapper, and an answering ache throbbed deep in her core. He knew his effect on her, and if he was trying to make her uncomfortable, it was working.

Shifting over, he opened up a hair's breadth of space between them. Because he sensed her discomfort, or because he couldn't bear to touch her. Now, she longed for his arms. When it was too late.

He rested his hands on his knees, still holding onto the card. For a moment, he said nothing. Just looked around the room. "Your suitcase exploded."

Was he scolding her for being messy or trying to lighten the mood? Had he not been scowling, she would guess he was teasing. She offered a lame excuse, which he could take any way he liked. "They won't stay shut."

"And the clothes won't stay in the suitcases?"

"It is odd how things slip out while I'm asleep."

He didn't smile, but his eyes appeared less flat. "You aren't used to picking up after yourself, are you?"

If he could banter with her, all was not lost.

"No." She sighed. "And I've realized I'm very lazy."

He tapped the card against his knee, staring off like his mind had drifted somewhere else. "Seeing as you're a famous actress, you must be rich. With servants to pick up the mess."

So, he was still with her, but he had stopped teasing. Evading his questions would be pointless. He held all the cards...or the one that mattered.

"My mother hired people to help with makeup and wardrobe, but I never had servants. Maybe at one time we were rich enough to afford them, but I don't know..."

Patrick stared at her with disbelief. "You don't know how much money you made?"

His tone implied she must be stupid. In hindsight, she had been. Stupid. Naïve.

"I never knew what we made. Mama always took care of financial matters, she kept the gold locked up in a steam trunk. Whatever I needed, she purchased."

"If your mother took care of you, why did you leave?"

Charm rubbed at her stinging eyes. "My mother died three months ago."

She had resisted crying, believing grief, and the acceptance that went with it, would worsen her fear of being alone. "I miss her...terribly. She took care of me. Maybe too much. Looking back, I can see I should've been more independent. Without her, it feels as if I've been set adrift in a leaky lifeboat."

"I'm sorry."

Did he mean he was sorry for her loss, or her belated insight? Whatever his meaning, his tone conveyed sympathy. His heart could be softening. Then again, the kind man she believed him to be wouldn't blackmail her. She had to discern his intentions before she gave away too much information. "Is it money you want?"

He shook his head.

How could she be sure when she didn't know him well enough to discern whether he would be truthful? "I want to believe you."

He looked down at her. The distant coldness in his

eyes melted into sadness. "I want to believe you, too."

She dropped her gaze before the tears welled. How hypocritical to question his trustworthiness after she'd deceived him.

Her toes dangled several inches above the floor. His booted feet were firmly planted. He easily had the strength to overcome her, even injured. Still, she wasn't afraid of him, had never been. He could have seduced her had he been persistent instead of giving her a wide berth, as she'd asked. Unlike Simon, Patrick had integrity, and the strength of character her father had lacked. In her heart, she knew he could be trusted. She wasn't as sure she could convince him to trust her.

First, she had to be more honest and open. "When I was four, maybe five, my father owned a concert saloon in San Francisco. Even then, I loved performing. He used to set me on the tables and I would sing and dance to entertain the miners. They called me Little Belle."

"La Belle Enfant," Patrick murmured in a thick Irish brogue. "The beautiful child."

"You know French?"

"Enough to translate that." He'd been holding the card face down. Now he turned it over. Revulsion rolled through her as she imagined what he must be thinking.

"I look like a whore."

"That's not what I see." His declaration eased her churning stomach. However, she couldn't read what was in his expression.

"What do you see?"

"An innocent, unaware of her seductive powers."

"That's a poetic way of putting it." She wouldn't mislead him. Not again. "I'm not innocent, Patrick, and I haven't been unaware since I was young enough to grasp what men meant by the things they whispered to each other…and sometimes to me."

He tossed the card, and her image landed in a

suitcase. She thought about closing the lid. Covering it up wouldn't change anything.

Patrick glowered, as if it offended him. Maybe that was his way of handling his disappointment in learning she wasn't pure. However repulsive or painful, the truth would be better for both of them. "Your father should've protected you."

How surprising his anger would be directed at her father instead of her. Her Papa had been even-tempered and fun loving, brilliantly witty, and protective in his own way. She loved him so much she couldn't condemn him for his flaws. "He didn't let anyone near me for as long as he lived. He died when I was fifteen. My mother protected me, too, although she encouraged the image. She told me I was only giving men what they wanted—an innocent they could lust after. That it was their sin, not mine. For a long time, I believed her."

"Not anymore?"

"No. That's why I won't wear the white dress. It makes me feel…filthy."

Patrick shifted closer. He put his arm around her, drawing her against his side. She should pull way rather than encourage him, and she would have if she had the willpower. Though there was nothing lurid or offensive about the way he touched her. He offered comfort because he was a good man with a compassionate heart, something she had seen in him from the start and couldn't resist. With Patrick, and only with Patrick, she felt truly accepted and cared for, like a person, not an object.

She gave in to her longing and rested her head against his shoulder.

He reached up and stroked her hair. "Why did you run away?"

"A few years after my father died, my mother met a man who owned a theater in St. Louis. Simon LaBar became my mother's lover, and then her husband and my manager. He arranged for me to perform in the best theaters, and had the contacts to get publicity wherever we went. He dictated the shows, the music, the dances, what I wore. Insisted on personally inspecting every costume."

"With you in it?"

"Yes. He said he wanted to see how well it fit." She had tried to tell herself he wasn't undressing her with his eyes. "My mother finally put a stop to it…a week before she died."

The muscles in Patrick's arm tensed. "That's why you ran? You thought he had something to do with her death?"

"The doctors said she had a weak heart. That's what killed her." Charm closed her eyes and willed her stomach to calm. If Simon had done something and she had missed picking up on it, she would never forgive herself. "I don't think he would murder her. He was her husband."

"That doesn't mean anything. Some men beat their wives."

"Simon didn't beat her. She would've left him. He didn't beat me, either."

"What did he do to you?" Patrick's voice resounded like a death knell.

She couldn't tell him, it was too humiliating, and no one would believe her. Everyone assumed actresses had loose morals. Patrick might think she invited the attention. There were other reasons she fled. "I found out after my mother died that he had managed to get complete control of our finances. He told me if I married him, he would take care of me…"

"So you ran."

"I thought if I went somewhere no one knew me, started over with a different name, Simon wouldn't find me."

Patrick didn't speak for long moment. She was glad he didn't take his arm away. If anything, he held her tighter.

She clung to his vest, which smelled of wool and tobacco smoke. Burrowing closer, she detected the scent of his warm skin. Clean, masculine, not masked by cloying fragrances. She ached to be closer, flesh-to-flesh, with nothing between them. Close enough she could forget about another man's hands on her.

"I'll protect you." His voice became husky, the brogue stronger. "Marry me, and LaBar can't touch you."

His heartfelt offer tempted her. Patrick would be a kinder master. Except, she didn't want another master, and she didn't want him tying himself down for her sake. Something inside her had been broken and couldn't be fixed. For that reason, she could never love him like he deserved to be loved.

"Thank you, Patrick. Your offer means more to me than I can express. But I can't accept. I won't let you bind yourself in a loveless marriage just so you can protect me."

He removed his arm. "Who said anything about love?"

Patrick left the bed. Remaining beside Charm would be unwise when every part of him ached to hold her, and never let go. She thought he'd come up here to shame her. Revenge wasn't what he sought. But coercing her into a marriage she didn't want would make him no better than that snake LaBar.

Charm hadn't told him everything, but he'd read into what she had said, and it made him sick, and furious.

She'd been a victim of the worst sort of man. No wonder she didn't trust his kind.

He tried to pace. Impossible without stepping on her clothes. Dresses and undergarments lay over the chair and bed, suitcases were open, spewing their contents onto the floor. The room seemed a reflection of her state of mind and situation—confused and messy. He liked order. Keeping things tidy gave him a sense of control. A false sense, of course. Few things were in his control, and Charm wasn't one of them.

That didn't change the fact she needed his protection. Even more than he first thought. He couldn't force her to accept him. She had to come to the decision of her own free will. In order for her to get there, she had to perceive the benefits of marriage. He would have to rely on the wisdom of others who'd been much smarter about relationships.

"My grandfather once told me, *People live in each other's shelter*."

"Another Irish saying?"

"Aye, we're very wise people. Where do you think Solomon got his proverbs?"

Her guarded expression dissolved into a smile. One barrier down. He didn't dare go over there and sit beside her, or he would have her in his arms and they would be right back where they'd started.

Needing a distraction, he kept his hands busy, picking up a child-sized boot with jet buttons down the side and searching out its mate. "We supposed to help each other, is what it means. I make my shelter next to yours..." Holding the shoes, he lifted his arms to demonstrate. "You make yours next to mine, and we form a bigger shelter. Get twice the benefit."

"Or one shoe each," she quipped.

"Keep your shoes. They won't fit me." He placed the tiny boots near the end of the bed.

Good, she was smiling and bantering with him, an improvement over suspicion. "I understand the basic principal, and it's a nice image, but you're the only one building a shelter, as far as I can see."

"That's not true. I give you my name and the protection marriage affords, and in exchange, you help me keep the saloon." He hated how selfish that sounded. But after being so hard on her for deceiving him, he refused to be dishonest. What he said was true, just not the only reason he wanted her.

"Keep the saloon?" She propped her hands on the side of the bed, regarding him with puzzlement. "I didn't know you were in danger of losing it."

"The brother of the man who sold me this place is contesting my claim. The railroad's policy gives married men priority. If I'm married, I'll stand a better chance at keeping my land." He bent down and moved the suitcase so he would have room to walk around.

Charm slid off the bed. She picked up a dress and walked over to the line of pegs near the door. Reaching high, she hung it up. Was this a sudden outbreak of neatness, or had he embarrassed her by tidying up? The last thing she needed was more guilt.

He grabbed the chair and pulled it over, straddled the cane seat and folded his arms over the back. No more picking up, and the chair would offer a wall of protection she might feel like she needed. "You'll be helping me, Charm. This isn't a one-sided deal I'm offering."

"Why me?" She picked up another dress and hung it by the first. "Why not ask one of the other women if you don't care who you marry."

"I do care—" He stopped his tongue before he blurted out just how much he cared. That would send her running because she didn't share his feelings. At the same time, he didn't want her to think his intentions were purely mercenary. "It wouldn't be fair to marry a woman who wants more than a marriage of convenience."

Charm had her back to him while she fiddled with arranging the dresses on the wall pegs. "Yes, you're right. They deserve more than that."

So do you. Patrick clamped his teeth shut to keep from blurting it out. That would give her an excuse not to marry him.

"What's your reason for not wanting a...a real marriage?" Her voiced sounded strained, but he couldn't see her face to read her emotions. He refused to talk to her back.

He set the chair aside. Aching with the need to comfort her, he cupped his hands on her shoulders.

She stiffened.

God, he longed to kill the man who'd hurt her and made her afraid.

"It's all right. I'm not going to do anything, I just want to show you something." With gentle insistence, he guided her to the window.

"You want to show me the view?"

"Best in town." He made the quip without feeling humorous. He hadn't practiced what he would say, only knew he had to lower his barriers so she would lower hers. Telling her about his failed marriage might not convince her to give the institution a try, but she'd risked honesty. Painful honesty. He owed her the same.

"The depot wasn't here when I first arrived three years ago. Neither was this building. My wife had to live in a sod house.

She turned her head sharply to look up at him.

"Surprised to hear I was married?"

"No, most men marry young...and you aren't young."

He laughed, more amused than offended by her blunt remark. When she decided to be honest, she didn't hold back. "No, I'm not young. But I'm not old, either, unless you consider thirty ancient."

"I'll be there in seven years, so no, I don't consider it old." Her gaze turned troubled, questioning. "You were telling me about your marriage."

"After the war, I wed a girl from New York, Kathleen Dooley. Her brother was in my company, one of the few who made it back..." Patrick paused at a wave of melancholy that blew in like dark clouds whenever he thought about the war. "Before we married, I told her of my plans to move west. She was excited, said it'd be a big adventure..."

"What happened to her?"

"She got out here and found she didn't like adventure. Hated the soddy, hated cooking over an open fire and washing her clothes in a creek. She was scared of the Indians and the wild creatures. She pined for her family and for her friends, and for the nice things she had when she lived in the city. Being her father's only daughter, she was used to being spoiled, and I didn't spoil her enough, or so she said. I promised her as soon as the railroad arrived, I'd build a place. But she wanted me to take her home. She didn't want to live in Kansas. I told her if we went back, we'd never have much. We'd be poor. The opportunity was out here, if she'd just be patient. She wasn't. She wanted her old life more than she wanted her new one. I took her as far as St. Louis and put her on a train. Six months ago, she wrote to tell me she had our marriage annulled. Claimed I couldn't give her children."

Charm put her hand on his arm in a comforting gesture "I'm sorry she left you."

He hadn't told her this to gain her sympathy. "She didn't leave. I let her go. I put her on the train instead of trying harder to make our marriage work. That's a mistake I won't make again."

The soft look in Charm's eyes encouraged him. He took a chance and reached for what he wanted. She allowed him to draw her into his embrace, and even put her arms around him. He buried his fingers in soft curls and pressed her head against his chest. To have her as his wife, the risk would be worth it. She might never come to love him. One day, she might decide to leave.

He wouldn't let her go without a fight. "We can be each other's shelter. Marry me, Juliette DuCharme."

She backed out of his arms. "I'm not that person anymore."

"All right, then, Charm…" He got down on one knee, an awkward position because of the pressure on his hip. Nevertheless, he'd do this properly, no matter how painful. "Will you do me the honor of becoming my wife?"

Her cheeks turned rosy. She tightened the sash on the quilted wrapper and nervously brushed loose hair out of her face. "I'm not dressed for a proposal."

"Put on a burlap sack, I wouldn't care."

Amusement eased the strain around her eyes and mouth. "You must be very worried about that other claim if you're willing to take me in a burlap sack."

He'd take her wearing nothing at all. Probably not the right thing to say.

She gazed out the window, deep in thought. "If I married, I'd want to maintain control over my money."

In light of what she'd told him, the demand wasn't surprising. Money wasn't the issue so much as trust. No matter what he said, she would doubt him, unless he gave her the proof she was looking for.

"We can sign an agreement that says your earnings are your own."

"You'd do that?" Her incredulous expression told him he was right about her lack of trust. She wouldn't believe he'd offer such a thing without a fair exchange.

"If you promise to stay with me...." *Forever.* No, he couldn't ask her to make a vow she wasn't ready to keep. "At least until I settle the claim on my land."

That would give him time to work on getting her to consider forever.

She hesitated. Then, with a look of determination, stuck out her hand. "We have a deal."

Chapter Eight

The wedding took place the next morning in the saloon in front of an itinerate preacher. Constantine and Rose Valentine stood as witnesses. The ceremony was blessedly brief. Afterwards Patrick poured a round of drinks, whiskey for the gentlemen and wine for the ladies.

Charm couldn't keep her hands from shaking. She was glad to have Rose beside her, even if her statuesque friend outshone her. Rose didn't put on airs. She didn't have a prideful bone in her body. Her husband adored her, as he should. Their courtship and marriage had been like something out of a fairy tale. Charm entertained no such fantasies. She had struck a deal with Patrick that was favorable to both of them, for as long as it lasted.

She took a sip of wine to calm her nerves.

Val raised his glass. "A toast to Patrick and Charm…to a lifetime of happiness."

A drop of wine trickled down her windpipe. She choked, and then coughed uncontrollably.

Patrick pounded her on the back. "Here now, you got to wait for the toasts before you start guzzling."

She narrowed her eyes. Her husband found her discomfort amusing? If she could catch her breath, she'd let him have it. The false vows they spoke in front of a Man of God, not to mention their best friends, were no laughing matter.

Rose took Charm's wine and exchanged it for water. "Take a sip, it'll help."

"Thank you," she choked out. While Patrick looked on—still smiling, the smug devil—she took small amounts of water. He'd probably put something in the wine. Some of Mr. Childers' deadly concoction.

"Let me add my congratulations, Mr. and Mrs. O'Shea." The Reverend Elijah Stillwater lifted his glass. "Good health, and a long life together."

"Hear, hear!" Patrick agreed heartily. He tossed back his drink.

Charm merely nodded her head. She still couldn't speak.

Her husband circled his arm around her waist and leaned in, kissing her cheek. "Better now?" he asked solicitously.

No, she wasn't better, and she wouldn't be better until everyone stopped talking about a long, happy marriage. Theirs would be neither.

Somehow, Patrick had convinced her that marrying him was the right thing to do. The argument had sounded rational at the time. Now, she wondered if she might've lost touch with reality. She likened being a wife in a temporary marriage to acting a part in a play. Soon, he would secure his land and she would have enough money to move on, and then the show would be over. Only, she'd gotten caught up in the illusion, speaking her vows as if she meant them. At least she hadn't worn the white dress. Her hypocrisy didn't extend that far.

"Give me a moment…" She walked away from her

husband, needing a moment alone to clear the confusion from her mind.

Rose came over to check on her. "Are you all right?"

"Yes, I'm fine. I just needed to clear my throat." The lie seemed to reassure her friend, and it was better than telling Rose the ceremony had been a farce.

"Aren't you wishin' we could kick up our heels?" Rose began to hum and sway to the music in her head, her leaf green skirt swirling around her feet. "You should've asked that nice Mr. Childers to bring his fiddle. He played at the last barn dance. Nobody sat down…"

"If Mr. Childers showed up, Patrick would put the fiddle over his head," Charm muttered.

"That's very funny. He's got no cause to be jealous with the way you look at him. Like he hung the moon…" Rose executed a twirl without spilling her wine.

Charm shook her head. Being in love had affected Rose's vision, as well as her good sense.

"I think it's romantic, how you and Mr. O'Shea met."

"Romantic?" Charm rolled her eyes. "Juliet's balcony scene is romantic. I applied for a job and had to force him to let me audition."

"He said you leapt into his arms."

"In a manner of speaking…" She supposed that might be considered romantic if they had fallen in love, which wasn't the case.

"Do you recall the day I married, and you loaned me garters?"

"I told you to keep them until the next marriage…" Charm turned her back on the men and drew up her skirt to reveal a red garter. "I didn't think I would be the one wearing them."

Rose lifted her glass. "To the Order of the Garter. You said we would stand by each other, come what may. Do you remember?"

Charm released a soft laugh. Her friend must think

marriage had affected her memory. "Of course I remember."

A look of melancholy fell over Rose's countenance. "I wish you'd invited our friends. I know you think they've shunned you, but I can't believe they meant it, and I know they'll be sorry they weren't here today."

She couldn't be serious. Wait, this was Rose, who saw the best in everyone.

Charm appreciated her friend's attempt to bring her back into the fold. In this case, however, her mother had been right. She shouldn't expect to form lasting friendships with those outside her circle, Rose being the exception. "They won't be sorry, I assure you. Besides, we wanted a simple ceremony."

Rose gave her a forgiving smile. Her heart was too full of love to hold grudges or spite or even unhappiness. "I'm glad you asked us to stand with you. Val says Patrick is a good man. I think you're perfect together."

"Perfect? I look like a dwarf standing next to him."

"Not a dwarf. Maybe a faery..." Rose's green eyes shone with amusement. "Wee faeries have been known to cast spells over mortals they take a fancy to."

More fairytales.

"Patrick isn't spellbound, believe me. He's a practical man. He's getting something out of this marriage, and so am I."

Rose regarded her with a puzzled look.

She didn't have the heart to tell her romantic friend that Patrick had only married her to secure his land. In a sense, it relieved her to know he didn't harbor unrealistic expectations. On the other hand, part of her—the soft, vulnerable part she dared not reveal—wished the fairy tale could be true.

"Come back and join the celebration," Patrick called out, and held up his glass. He gave her a smile that deepened the adorable dimples in his cheeks. The knowing looks he'd been sending her all day made her heart race and her hands tremble.

Before the wedding, he'd whispered in her ear about how much he looked forward to their wedding night. Heaven help her, so did she. She shouldn't worry, he'd told her. He knew she wasn't virginal, so his assurance must have something to do with his not being able to sire children. That being the case, she wouldn't have to worry about getting with child. She should be glad they wouldn't have that concern. So why did the thought of not carrying his child make her sad?

"Your husband is wanting you by his side…" Rose pointed out with a teasing smile.

"It won't hurt him to wait."

Her friend's smile vanished. "Is something troubling you, Charm?

Was it so obvious?

"No, I'm just a bit overwhelmed…" And fearful of what her heart was telling her, that she'd spoken vows she wanted to keep, but couldn't.

Patrick and Val stood near the bar, chatting with the dark-haired preacher who looked to be about the same age. He'd performed the wedding ceremony for Val and Rose. Someone, maybe Hope, had told her that he didn't have a church. Maybe he would stay and they would build him one. Centralia could use more peaceful men.

"Thank you for coming here to marry us." Patrick shook the preacher's hand.

"My privilege." Stillwater looked around, as if noticing the interior for the first time. "This is a nice place. How many people will it seat?"

"We got over a hundred in here for Charm's debut," Patrick answered.

"A hundred?" The preacher made a quick study of the stage behind him. "Would you let me use the space for church services on Sundays?"

Charm covered a smile so she wouldn't offend him by laughing. The only congregants were likely to men expecting to slake their thirst after a heated sermon.

"Why not? We're closed for business on Sundays anyway." Patrick shook hands with the preacher—who didn't ask him to sign anything.

Her husband had offered to put their agreement in writing. She knew he'd done it solely to ease her mind. Patrick would honor his promises, regardless. His word was his vow.

Charm stared at him, stricken by a sudden realization. His vows. He'd spoken them in a firm, confident voice, swearing to honor and cherish her and to cleave to her—until death.

Her heart quivered as Cupid's arrow found its mark. Was it possible? Did he truly love her, and that was why he'd made those vows?

She scoffed at the fanciful notion. He'd never confessed to such a thing. What, then, was his motive for wanting to keep her? Holding onto the golden goose, of course.

The cheerful conversation around her seemed to come from far away, a buzzing in her head. Charm trembled as Patrick's arm came around her. He drew her against him in a gesture both tender and possessive. "You're being awfully quiet. That concerns me..."

"It should."

Stubborn Irishman. He'd tricked her into thinking their marriage would be temporary. She should've known better after he'd told her the story about letting his wife go and not making the same mistake. How did he think he could prevent her from leaving? The only thing that would make it difficult, if not impossible to leave, would be if she had a...

Child.

Her chest grew tight as panic set in. How could she

have a child if he couldn't...? What were his exact words? He never said his wife's accusation was true, only that she used it as an excuse for an annulment.

Patrick leaned down and put his lips by her ear. "Are you nervous, is that what's bothering you? It's all right to be nervous on your wedding day. I'll admit to being a wee bit nervous, too."

Nervous wasn't the right word. She couldn't find words to describe her heartbreak. Hadn't she known all along that Patrick wouldn't have to use force to bend her to his will? He'd wooed her with tenderness. Thoughtful gestures.

She reached up, and fondled the silk ribbons on the bonnet he'd given her, *a token of his regard*. The sweet gesture had touched her deeply, and she'd insisted on wearing his gift at their wedding. That he'd manipulated her emotions was bad enough. Worse, she had fooled herself into believing she could marry him and keep her heart unbound.

He held her close to his side with his arm wrapped around her, offering protection. She leaned into his shoulder, unable to resist the lure. He could give her things she longed for almost as much as her freedom. A safe shelter and a place to belong. In the end, it was a snare. He would use her love to cage her. She'd be a well-fed songbird.

Sadly, he might not think he'd done anything wrong. He was a man, after all, and men only wanted two things from women: sex and total submission. He tried to pretend that wasn't what he wanted, but tonight, she would force him to admit the truth.

After everyone left and Patrick locked up, he ducked

beneath the bar to retrieve something he'd hidden away for this special occasion. Gaining Charm's agreement to marry him hadn't been easy. The bigger challenge—dismantling her defenses—was still to come. He would start tonight.

Whistling one of Charm's cheery tunes, he withdrew a bottle and two goblets.

"What? More wine?" Charm drifted over beside him. Her floral fragrance teased his senses. From perfume she wore or the flowers woven through her hair? She leaned in, and her breast pressed against his arm.

Desire roared through him. Somehow, he managed not to fumble while he uncorked the bottle and poured. He handed her a glass. "French Cognac. Your favorite, I believe."

She lowered her lashes and took a dainty sip. "Mmm, it's delicious. Where did you find it?"

"In the back, where I keep all my expensive liquor."

"And you withheld it from me, shame on you."

"Saved it, for a special occasion." He poured a small amount into his goblet, would savor a mouthful, but no more. "After your first performance, I brought the bottle up to your room to share a toast. You were…indisposed."

A blush stained her cheeks. "I was tired."

"Tired of putting up with me, you mean."

Her eyes rounded with feigned innocence. "Why would you say that?"

"To my adorable little wife…" He clinked his glass against hers. "You heard me knocking. Loud enough to raise the dead."

She took another sip and licked her lips. "If I'd known you had French Cognac, I would've roused from my deathlike slumber."

"Are you sufficiently roused now?" With a wicked smile, he set his glass on the bar. Play now. Drink later.

Her eyes widened with a look of alarm; tipping her goblet, she finished off the cognac. He'd never seen her gulp drinks until today, so he assumed she was nervous. The brandy would relax her, before he took her to bed. She set her empty glass on the bar, without the saucy smile. "We need to talk..."

"Talking isn't what I had in mind." He tried to slip his arm around her waist, but she evaded capture by sidestepping and handing him the goblet he'd put down.

"You aren't drinking?"

He set the stemmed glass aside. "I've had enough."

Her gaze flickered to her empty goblet, and the blush in her cheeks deepened. "So have I, it would seem."

She mistakenly thought he disapproved of her indulgence. He needed to explain, but in explaining, he would have to reveal some things about himself. Things she ought to know anyway, considering she was his wife. If he didn't confess, she would figure it out soon enough.

He refilled her glass. "Have as much as you like. The reason I'm not drinking..." He shifted his weight to his good leg. Nothing she'd said or done would lead him to believe she would despise him for his weakness, but he still feared telling her. "If I drink on top of the medicine I take, it'll put me to sleep." He offered a lop-sided grin. "And I'm not ready to go to sleep."

She looked down at his bad leg. When her eyes lifted, they shone with empathy. "You never told me how you were injured."

This was bound to come up sometime. He just wished that sometime wasn't now. "It happened during the war."

"You were a soldier?"

"Aye...a reluctant one."

"Drafted?"

"Not exactly... Me and me brother, we were

116

recruited fresh off the boat while we still had stars in our eyes. They told us we'd get our meals free, and on top of that, good pay. Made it sound like Christmas. By the time we realized what we'd signed up for, it was too late."

She looked into her glass, her frown thoughtful. "Where is your brother now?"

"Dead." Patrick said it quick, like yanking out a thorn. A flash of pain, and then it was over. Except, he wasn't over his brother's death, and never would be. That wound wouldn't heal any better than the injury to his leg.

He heaved a resigned sigh. Might as well have done with the explanation, and then he wouldn't need to talk about it again, and especially not on a night meant for beginnings, not endings.

"At Fredericksburg, it was…" He stared into the past. Once again, smelling the acrid smoke, hearing the echoes of dying men's screams, tasting the sharp tang of fear. "We charged the Rebs. Ran straight at 'em while they were hunkered down behind a stone fence. They picked us off, as easy as shooting ducks sitting on a pond."

Sweat beaded on his upper lip. The rhythm of the drum sounded in his eyes…or was that his heartbeat? "We advanced over the bodies of our dead and wounded with our commander screamin', *'Faugh-a-bellagh!'* *Clear the way!* A shell exploded behind me. The force knocked me into the air. It killed Michael right off, though I didn't know it until later…" He hadn't been able to retrieve his younger brother's body to give him a proper burial. Michael's remains had been tossed into a mass grave.

Should've been him that died, seeing as it was his idea to sign on in the first place. Over and over, he'd played in his mind the different choices he should've made.

Grief thickened in Patrick's throat. Charm's face, drawn with concern, wavered. He blinked away the tears and coughed to clear this throat, so he could finish the story without his voice cracking. "The metal tore into my right hip and lower back. The sawbones told me they dug out everything they could find. Still feels like there's something inside… All the doc can do is give me opium to ease the pain. It blunts me senses, so I've been trying to take less. But I've got a hunger for it now…"

Seeing his pain reflected in his wife's gaze dragged him back to the present.

"I can't bear to think about how much it must've hurt to lose your brother, and the pain, always with you," she whispered, with big fat tears rolling down her cheeks.

He knew this was a bad time to talk. Using the sides of his thumbs, he wiped her cheeks and tried to make light of a dismal subject. "It's a reminder not to expect a leprechaun to pop out of nowhere and offer me a pot of gold."

"You mean you learned not to trust people."

That wasn't what he wanted her to take from this conversation because he needed her to trust him, in spite of what life had taught her. "I learned I wasn't as lucky as I thought."

She reached up and took his hand, turned her face into his palm and kissed it. "You're alive. That's my good luck."

With that, she would've snared his heart, if he hadn't already given it to her.

"I'm glad you think so." The fullness in his chest from all the emotions that had been churned up made it difficult to talk. Words wouldn't express what he felt anyway. He had to show her.

He untied the knot on the sheer shawl wrapped around her shoulders. With his finger he traced her jaw, lifting her chin before he bent down and put his lips on the spot where her pulse throbbed. When she gasped, he wrapped his arm around her waist so she couldn't escape and trailed kisses across her collarbone. The low-necked dress showed off her petite form to perfection. He couldn't wait to peel away her clothing and kiss every inch of her satiny skin.

A desperate need drove him. The need to affirm life, and to show her the things he'd hoarded in his heart.

"P-Patrick," she stammered in a breathless voice. "I don't think we should—"

"Then don't think…" Returning to her mouth, he captured her lips. He wanted her senses engaged, not her brain. He couldn't talk her into falling in love with him.

They hadn't discussed what came after the ceremony. She had to know. That didn't mean she would be any less nervous. He circled her waist with his hands. She was so tiny. He'd have to be careful. Gentle. Maybe the disparity in their sizes intimidated her.

He lifted her and set her on the bar, which brought her closer to eye level.

She blinked slowly, appearing dazed, which he interpreted as progress. Encouraged, he touched a small purple flower tucked within a curl.

"Whose idea was this?

"Rose helped me dress my hair. She brought the flowers."

"I'll have to remember to thank her." He tugged the heavy skirts higher, ran his hands up her stocking-clad legs to her knees and gently opened them so he could move in closer and put his arms around her…bring his lips to hers… An added benefit, he could kiss her without getting a crick in his neck.

She returned his kisses, shyly at first, and then with more eagerness, even urgency. Her restless hands toyed with his hair, combing, stroking. Her touch sent waves of pleasure crashing over him. When she drew him closer, he gave in to the hunger eating him alive.

Cradling her head in his hands, he plundered her mouth. Cognac and lavender, tastes and smells he would always associate with his wife, with this moment. He fished for the pins that held the hair in an elaborate coiffure. As he removed them, flowers rained down on his arms.

Liquid fire coursed through his veins, filling him with a sense of power and the overwhelming urge to mate.

His hands shook as he undid the pearl buttons down the front of her gown. Pulling the sleeves over her arms, he pressed fervent kisses on her neck and shoulders. He didn't intend to consummate their marriage on the bar, but there was no reason he couldn't pleasure her before he took her upstairs. He tugged at the silk ribbon holding the neckline of her camisole together, and touched the swell of her breasts. Small, but perfectly formed.

"Patrick, no…" She tugged his hair, momentarily pulling him off course like the wind whipping at a sail. Still nervous, but she'd get over it, as soon as he had her undressed and laid out before him like a buffet dinner.

"I said *no!*" She seized his hands.

His attention veered. He blinked, coming out of the sensual daze. She'd stopped him…why? Might have something to do with being stripped on top of a bar. He squeezed her hands and pressed a tender kiss on her forehead. "We can go upstairs," he murmured.

"We can't do this."

Can't. Do. This. Her words took a moment to sink in. Even then, it didn't make sense. Of course they could *do this*. They were married, *this* is what married folks did.

She pulled her hands out of his grasp and gripped the sagging camisole in tight fists. "I'm not ready."

He took in her mussed hair, flushed face and full lips

still damp from his kisses. She looked ready. Except for her eyes, which were dark, fearful.

Clumsy oaf. He'd mauled her and frightened her when he should've slowed down and taken his time. He combed his fingers through her loosened hair, taking great care not to tug or pull.

"A chuisle mo chroí," he said hoarsely. *Pulse of my heart.* Truly, she was, even if she wasn't ready to hear it just yet. He cupped her cheek. "I'll be gentle with you."

Her lips quivered. "I know…"

"If you know, then why are you afraid?"

"Because I know what you want…what you really want."

What he wanted? Wasn't it obvious? He wanted *her.* Though he sensed she wasn't referring to his immediate needs. He frowned, uneasy. "You're talking in riddles. Tell me straight what it is you think I want."

She pulled up the sleeves and held her dress in place. Narrowed her eyes, accusingly. "You want to bind me to you with a child. I thought you couldn't give me children. But then I realized that's what you wanted me to think…"

Sadness weighed down on him, creating a soul-deep ache worse than the constant pain racking his body. He couldn't convince her that he loved her if she believed he was the kind of man who would enslave her. She mistook his intentions, though he could think of nothing more wonderful than having a child with her. That she considered it bondage broke his heart.

He dropped his hands to his sides. "If that's what you think, I'm surprised you married me."

Her frown reflected hurt more than anger. "You told me you wanted a mutually beneficial arrangement. One that wasn't permanent, that's…that's what you told me."

Deny it or make excuses. Lies would only confirm her low opinion of him. He did want to keep her, and planned to bed her to show her just how much he wanted her to stay; and he hadn't given a thought as to what might happen if she became pregnant.

Now, if he admitted to loving her, she wouldn't believe him. All he could hope for was that she might want the same thing he did. If not, he couldn't...he wouldn't...force her to lie with him. Nor would he seduce her and make her distrust love even more.

"What do *you* want, Charm?"

Her suspicion frustrated him.

"It's a simple question. I'm not trying to trick you. You say you know what I want, but I'm not so sure what you want. That's why I'm asking."

She bit her lip, appearing distraught. Then she lifted her chin, challenging him with hurt in her eyes. "What I told you before. I want to go back to acting, traveling and performing."

That pretty well put the nail in the coffin. She didn't want to be with him enough to stay here and perform. She wanted a better theater, a bigger audience...and why not, she was a famous actress, not some gifted hopeful, as he'd first assumed.

"It seems you and I want different things." He lifted her off the bar and set her on her feet.

"You're right. I do want you to stay with me, and I hoped to convince you. But you're wrong about one thing. I won't bed you in order to trap you. You're free to leave whenever you want."

Chapter Nine

Charm slept apart from her husband on her wedding night. It wasn't because he'd admitted his intention to keep her, or because she didn't trust him not to use underhanded methods. He had given her what she wanted. Freedom. She should feel good.

She didn't. She was miserable.

His tender seduction had confused her and made her think he might actually have strong feelings for her. When she confronted him about his deceit, she hoped he would have a reason, and his reason would be that he loved her and couldn't live without her. But he only confessed to wanting to keep her, and then set her free.

She tossed and turned, and more than once got out of bed and considered going across the hall. That would seal her fate. Once she crawled into bed with him and joined her body with his, it would be impossible to leave. Being that vulnerable, that intimate, she would never be able to protect her heart.

When daylight tiptoed into her room, she could barely crack her eyes open.

After crawling out of bed, she found a note on the

floor near the door. As she read Patrick's bold script, her spirits went into a downward spiral.

I've gone to meet with Mr. Hardt about my claim and intend to resolve the issue.

In other words, if he was successful, she could leave sooner. Tears burned behind her eyelids. She blinked them away and finished reading.

You'll find breakfast in the kitchen.

His thoughtful gesture knifed her conscience. She had accused him of being selfish. There wasn't a more generous man around than Patrick O'Shea.

She found his door unlocked, so she ventured inside.

Silence greeted her, along with a mouth-watering smell. Fresh bread.

A folded newspaper and magazines were stacked on a table next to a stuffed chair. The cushion had a permanent dip in the middle, indicating it was his favorite place to sit and read. When she'd first met him, she'd judged him to be messy and uncouth because of his rustic attire and bushy beard.

How wrong she'd been.

On the kitchen table, she found a basket with bread, a jar of jam and fresh strawberries. He couldn't possibly know they were her favorite. She took a bite, releasing the juicy sweetness with a moan of pure pleasure. This wasn't the first time he made sure she had something good to eat. He fed her regularly, and well, and he saw to it that she had a safe place to stay.

Though he'd wed her and had every right to expect her to share his bed, he hadn't forced his attentions on her. He'd been gentle, even with his seduction, never pushing her further than she was comfortable, letting her set the pace. When she'd resisted, he stopped, and made it clear he wouldn't trick her into sleeping with him, or staying. He gave her the choice. Those weren't the actions of a self-serving manipulator.

After she finished eating and cleaned up, she hurried down the stairs, her mood greatly improved by the strawberries and the insight she'd gained. Her assumptions about his motives had been wrong because she hadn't looked through the eyes of love. She had viewed him through a lens of fear, which distorted the truth. Patrick cared for her, possibly loved her. Even if he hadn't declared it, he showed it in many ways.

After she had rejected him and accused him of deceit, he might've decided to give up. But she wasn't giving up. There was still a chance to work things out, and she would tell him she wanted to try. That would be a start.

The saloon remained empty. Chairs were turned upside down and stacked on tables to make it easier to sweep. She walked by the bar and ran her fingers along the surface. Clean, of course. Patrick took good care of his place. He also took good care of her.

"We can be each other's shelter."

When he issued his unique proposal, she thought she understood, but she hadn't grasped the full meaning. Given the struggles he faced—the chronic pain, his dependency on opium, the daily challenges of carving out a life on a rough frontier—he needed her for more than her acting ability. He needed her sheltering arms as much as she needed his. Maybe more.

All her life, people had needed for her talent, not for her love. Patrick needed her love.

She leapt onto the stage. How marvelous, miraculous even, that Providence had brought her to this place, to this man. She had a lifetime of love stored up, just waiting for the day when she could give it to someone who wanted it, needed it.

Dancing with pure joy, she celebrated. They still had things to work out—his business, her career, their future—but they would do it together, beneath each other's shelter.

At the sound of the door closing, she whirled around with a smile on her face, expecting to see her husband. Instead, she saw the Devil, disguised in a fashionable three-piece suit and top hat. "Simon!"

Startled while coming out of a pirouette, she stumbled, and had to throw out her arms to regain her balance and avoid falling on her face. Her heart galloped, but not from the brief exercise. "How…how did you find me?"

Amusement gleamed in black eyes that haunted her nightmares. His thin lips curved into a slight smile. "Give me some small credit for having intelligence enough to track you down. I knew you'd taken a train. It just took a little longer to find out you signed up to be a bride. I didn't expect that. Surprisingly creative."

Charm took a step back. He wasn't close yet, but just seeing him in the same room triggered an overpowering urge to run. How she had at one time thought of him as a surrogate father, she couldn't imagine. She'd as soon curl up next to a rattlesnake. Come to think of it, a snake would've made a better guardian. At least it would've issued a warning before striking. Simon had waited until after her mother's funeral, when she was at her weakest, to make his move. When he struck, she'd been unprepared and unable to fight him off.

He strolled to the center of the room, removing spotless white gloves. Unlike Patrick, Simon's cleanliness went no deeper than the surface. "I must say I didn't expect to find you playing the part of a saloon girl."

She hoped he wouldn't find her at all. Had counted on having more time to prepare to face him, and to overcome her fear and the sense of being helpless. Trapped.

Wait, he couldn't trap her. She was beyond his reach.

"I'm not a saloon girl. I am an entertainer—and I'm

married." So there! He could chew on that. Hopefully, choke on it. He couldn't undo what was done, and as Patrick had promised, she would be safe.

"Is that so? Then congratulations are in order." Simon's unperturbed reaction took her aback. She anticipated surprise at the very least, and anger. He showed neither. "If you offered me a drink, we could toast your matrimonial bliss and drink to the good health of your husband, Mr. O'Shea."

She caught a sharp breath. Impossible. He couldn't know her husband. Had they met, Patrick would've suspected a stranger who was looking for her. That meant Simon had been snooping around, asking questions. This frightened her more than his sudden appearance. "What...what do you know of Mr. O'Shea?"

Simon lifted one shoulder in an unconcerned shrug. "I know he's an Irish immigrant, and that he deserted his post—"

"That's a lie!" Her face flushed hot with outrage. "My husband served honorably."

"Is that the story he told? Did he also tell you he was jailed for getting into fights? Seems your Irishman has a hot temper." Simon's gaze filled with sad rebuke. "Really, Juliette, I thought you had better taste."

She took a firm grip on her soaring temper. It should come as no surprise that he would disparage her husband, or any man he saw as his competition. She stood straighter, prouder, refusing to listen to his lies. "I have excellent taste, which is why I married Mr. O'Shea—"

The falsehood caught in her throat. That wasn't why she'd married Patrick. Even as late as last night, the first evening of their marriage, she'd lost faith in him and had questioned his motives. Yes, but he wasn't the fickle one. She'd let him believe her heart wasn't involved.

She didn't deserve as fine a man as her husband, even if she'd decided he was the man she wanted.

Simon stroked the beard he kept trimmed and oiled. She recalled the spicy pomade he used on his hair, and her stomach turned. "It is a curiosity. Why you married him, that is. He isn't rich, or well connected. He does have this fine establishment. Though I hear he may not have it for long."

The satisfaction glittering in his eyes sent a chill down her spine. She'd seen that look before. He had some devilish plan.

She darted a frantic look at the nearest table. If she leapt down and turned it over, or threw a chair, she might get past him and out the door.

Even if escape were possible, the problem wouldn't go away. Simon would come after her. Remembering how Patrick had responded to Mr. Childers' innocent flirting, she could imagine what he'd do if Simon confronted him.

No, she couldn't run to Patrick and invite disaster. She would never be free of Simon if she didn't face her fears.

She drew up straight, braced her hands on her hips and looked him in the eye. "I am a married woman now. We will have nothing more to do with each other. You need to leave."

Simon's smile didn't falter. "It's time to stop playacting, my dear. You've had your fun, and I'm willing to forgive and forget this ever happened. If you'll come along like a good girl."

Revulsion rolled over her in a hot wave. He'd told her to be a good girl and to mind him whenever he wished to visit her dressing room, to be a good girl and give him her virginity, to be a good girl and marry him, so he could do as he pleased, anytime he pleased.

"I'm not going anywhere with you," she shouted,

fisting her hands. Resentment whipped up a storm of fury. "You have no control over me anymore... I *despise* you!"

He didn't blink when she hurled her hatred at him. "How you feel about me is irrelevant. You entered into an agreement. Or have you forgotten?"

His cold declaration had the same effect as a bucket of freezing water thrown in her face.

"My agreement...?" Did he mean the one that made him her manager? She should've paid more attention to the stipulations, but she'd been unprepared to be on her own and he had taken advantage of her. She owed him nothing. "I'm starting over. Our agreement doesn't apply anymore."

"That's where you're wrong." Reaching inside his coat, he pulled out a creased paper, unfolded it and held it up. "This is a judge's order that compels you to return and fulfill the remainder of your contract term. If you choose to breach your agreement, you must pay me five thousand dollars."

A tremor struck and the earth shifted, or maybe it was just her world that crumbled beneath her feet. She expected Simon to come after her, but hadn't anticipated he would find her so quickly, or have the power of the legal system behind him. "I don't have five thousand dollars."

Simon held out his arms with a benign smile. "Then come back and honor your contract. That's all I ask."

He must think her a stupid fish with that lure.

"I told you, I'm not going back with you."

"That would be a poor decision..." He shook his head, feigning sadness. "If you refuse to cooperate, I'll be forced to ask the authorities to intervene."

Her heart drummed retreat. She had to remain strong. "You can't force me to go with you. I'll fight you in court."

Simon folded the order and returned it to his pocket. "Be my guest. You can plot your strategy from a jail cell. I'm sure any judge will agree you can't be trusted not to run."

Fear twisted her stomach into knots. She knew from personal experience that Simon would carry through with his threats. He had connections with crooked politicians and judges who owed him favors, and she'd learned first-hand how ruthless he could be.

"Your husband could cover your debt," he said smoothly.

She flushed with shame at how quickly her desperate mind grasped at the idea. Patrick wouldn't hesitate because he was an honorable man, but coming up with five thousand dollars would bankrupt him. He still had to pay off what he owed on the building, the land. There had to be another way. "I'm not involving my husband."

"What makes you think you have a choice in the matter? When O'Shea married you, he took on your commitments, which means he is now responsible for what you owe." Simon drew his gloves through his palm. She stared with horror, recalling how he'd done that, over and over, as he'd described in detail how he planned to humiliate her when she resisted his advances, as if she had no more power to resist than a pair of limp gloves. "If you refuse to fulfill your contractual obligations, I shall be forced to file a lawsuit to recover my losses from your Mr. O'Shea."

The words fell like blows.

God forgive her for dragging Patrick into the mess she'd made of her life. She hadn't anticipated this was what Simon would do, and because of her shortsightedness her husband would be punished along with her.

That was Simon's plan. He didn't just want her

returned to him. Oh no, that wouldn't satisfy. He intended to hurt the man who'd been kind to her and had offered her his name and protection even when she didn't deserve it.

If she sought Patrick's help, he would stand by her...and be ruined in the process. Everything he'd worked for would be taken away. If she left, he would believe she didn't trust him and would never know how she really felt about him. Oh, impossible choice! The only way to save her husband would be to leave him. Hurt him in order to protect him.

Pain wrung her heart. She loved Patrick. Even if he never knew it, and ended up despising her, she couldn't let him suffer for her mistakes.

But to go with Simon? A shudder went through her. She would run to the ends of the earth to avoid him...and would leave destruction in her wake. The only way to end his hold on her would be to work out her contract and be done with him.

Squaring her shoulders, she faced him. "If I return, it is for the sole purpose of completing this cursed contract. We will have nothing else to do with each other. And I want you to sign an agreement that says neither I nor my husband owe you anything else."

Simon spread his hands in acquiescence. "Of course. All I ask is that you honor your contract. Once you're finished, you can do as you please."

He lied, of course. He would do whatever he could to keep her. He'd already tried coercion, seduction, even rape. The hair on her arms and on the back of her neck prickled. She hadn't fought back before. Fear had made her his victim. She was stronger now. If he touched her again, she would kill him.

She darted a glance at the door. Should her husband return and find Simon here, there was no telling what he would do. Something that would get him arrested, no doubt. Which meant she had to act quickly. "Let me pack my things, and I'll meet you at the station."

"I'll help you collect them." Simon pulled a watch from his vest pocket and consulted the time. "If we hurry, we can make the next train."

"Exercise patience, O'Shea." Ross Hardt set aside a document he'd signed and shuffled through a stack of papers on his desk. He frowned as he turned over a sheet. "Hmm. I know that letter is here somewhere…"

Patrick stretched his aching leg and heaved a frustrated sigh. Saints preserve him. Sitting was worse than standing, and he'd been planted in this chair for over an hour, answering questions about his agreement with Gilly, providing dates, names of witnesses. He'd grown tired of being patient. However, winning Charm required patience. He may well have lost her because he got impatient and pushed her into marriage. Had he exercised restraint, he might've been able to convince her he loved her and they wouldn't be at odds.

He groused at Hardt, having no one else to target. "Patience be damned. The railroad had my paperwork for over a year. McGill didn't show up until the other day. Why do you have to consider his request? There's got to be some time limit, or something…"

"That doesn't apply to railroad land."

Patrick harrumphed. "The railroad is above the law, that's what you're saying."

Hardt glanced up from his writing. "No. I'm correcting your misperception about limitations on land claims."

"Well, I'm married now, so that's no obstacle…" Patrick didn't mention he hadn't consummated the union. Something he planned to correct as soon as he convinced Charm he wasn't out to trap her. Her accusations stung. Despite knowing he'd brought about her wrath by not being honest about his feelings for her. He'd feared rejection. Now, he might've lost her anyway.

He shifted in the seat, fighting the melancholy that pulled at him like quicksand. Withdrawing a handkerchief from his back pocket, he mopped his forehead. Hardt hadn't broken a sweat, so it must not be the heat. Could be nervousness, or the result of withholding the medicine. After admitting to his hunger for opium, he'd decided he would cut back. He'd seen what the irresistible craving had done to former warriors, and he refused to become one of those pathetic creatures. His wife deserved better. He could live with pain easier than he could live with dishonor.

"Give me time to finish my investigation." Hardt placed his pen in the inkwell. He rubbed his fingers together, which only smeared ink from his forefinger onto his thumb. "Didn't leak last night." He withdrew a handkerchief and wiped at the smudge. "Congratulations, by the way. You made the right decision by marrying that girl."

"Yeah. Hopefully, she'll feel the same way soon," Patrick muttered, as he heaved himself out of the chair. He'd accomplish nothing further by sitting here.

He eyed Hardt's black fingers and messy desk. "Why don't you hire an assistant to help you get organized? It's a wonder you can find anything."

"No one wants the job."

"Doesn't surprise me," Patrick conceded. Working at the land office would be a sure-fire way to become the most unpopular person in town.

Hardt stood and picked up his coat from the back of the chair. He stepped around the desk. "I'll walk with you. Have to take the train to Fort Scott. The directors want a status report on the brides." He sighed and shook his head.

Patrick didn't envy the agent's responsibility even though he was pretty sure he wouldn't have done anything as stupid as suggesting a bride lottery. The railroad's immigration program had sounded good at first. But things hadn't turned out as expected. For one, there weren't enough women to go around. Hardt's recommended solution had only worsened the problem. Not only did the settlers hate him, now the women resented him as well.

Hardt peered out the window. He turned abruptly and went back to his desk. "I forgot something. We'll talk later..."

Patrick grabbed his hat on the way out, anxious to get back to the saloon and check Charm's temperature. Still chilly, or had she warmed up? He hoped she'd found his note and his peace offering—fresh strawberries.

Just outside the door, he stopped to greet two women passing by, among the last of the prospective brides to remain unwed. It had turned into something of a game amongst the men in town to see who could corral the next one.

"Good morning, Mr. O'Shea." Mrs. Braddock's smile didn't reach her eyes.

Patrick tipped his hat politely. "And to you, ma'am."

He assumed the widow blamed him for corrupting Charm. He wasn't too happy with these ladies, either, for abandoning their friend when she needed them.

The pretty widow glanced around him at the picture window.

"Mr. Hardt's in there, if you need to speak with him."

She jerked her attention back to his eyes, blushing. "I'm not looking for Mr. Hardt."

Another popular game, betting on which of the two

would win the ongoing war between the feisty widow and the land agent. Her first day town, Mrs. Braddock had reportedly slapped Hardt for some infraction. He might've seen her coming and decided to delay leaving his office until she was gone. Funny, he didn't have the reputation for being a coward.

The other prospective bride stepped forward, dressed entirely in black and hugging a black shawl. Grim-looking woman. "You may not remember me, Mr. O'Shea. I'm Prudence Walker."

She was right. He didn't remember her.

"Congratulations on your marriage..." She hesitated.

"Thank you."

"Would you convey our best wishes to your wife?"

Trying to pretend politeness, eh? He wouldn't play into her hands. "Come by and offer them yourself. I'm sure Mrs. O'Shea would appreciate seeing a friendly face."

Mistress Prudence blanched. At the thought of entering a saloon, no doubt. She clutched the shawl tighter. "I would love to see her. But she moved out of the hotel, and we understood she didn't want to be bothered."

Either the Plain Jane was a liar, or she'd misunderstood. Patrick aimed to set things straight and tweak their noses in the process. "She didn't leave. he was evicted; and as far as I know, she never told anybody not to come see her."

"How can that be?" The widow demanded.

"Mrs. Fry *lied* to us, that's how." Miss Walker's eyes flashed with indignation. "She's the one who told us Charm decided to leave and wanted nothing more to do with us."

Mrs. Braddock's lips thinned. "Then we will move out. I refuse to stay somewhere one of my friends isn't welcomed."

Patrick found the exchange enlightening. If true, he'd

be having a talk with those hotel owners. They owed his wife an apology, at the very least. He tucked the information away until he could do something about it. In the meantime, he felt he had to warn the ladies not to act too rashly. "There aren't any other rooms in town. No place acceptable for ladies."

"We'll see about that." Mrs. Braddock started for the door to the land office. "Mr. Hardt should be informed. We'll demand that he find us other lodgings."

Oh, that ought to please the land agent to no end.

Patrick took the cue to escape. "Sounds like a good idea. I'll leave you to it."

"Tell Charm we miss her...and we'll stop in soon for a visit..." Miss Walker's voice followed him. He didn't imagine she would risk her reputation to come to a saloon, but he would let Charm know her friends wanted to see her.

He passed by the depot where a train waited amidst clouds of smoke and steam. Those determined ladies might detain Hardt. Seeing as he was the highest-ranking railroad official in the area, the engineer would hold the train for him.

The last passengers boarded, including a couple entering the parlor car directly behind a private railcar reserved for Hardt. A fancy gent opened the door for a petite young woman in a blue traveling suit. From the back, she resembled Charm.

She disappeared inside the railcar before Patrick could get a good look at her.

Unease rippled through him. What if it was Charm?

Ridiculous. Why would she be getting on a train with some stranger?

Unless he wasn't a stranger...

Patrick squelched his suspicion. He wouldn't let jealousy make him act like a fool...again. He stepped into the street, leaving the train behind.

Knowing Charm, she was probably still in bed. Wasn't even noon yet. Maybe he'd join her... He smiled at the thought.

His little wife turned his well-ordered world upside down with her crazy sleeping habits, her untidiness, her energetic drive and big ideas. Everything about her would seem to be the opposite of what he needed. But he'd gotten stuck, and Charm had pulled him out of a rut. She'd reawakened the man he didn't think still existed.

For years, he'd been waiting, hoping his luck would change. Time he made his own luck and went after an impossible dream, like those he had when he left Ireland and came to America. He would tell Charm that he loved her, and challenge her to face her feelings for him. They were meant for each other. Why, it couldn't be clearer.

Inside the saloon, McLaughlin rattled around behind the bar, helping himself to a shot of whiskey.

"What the hell are you're doing?"

The intruder gave him a sheepish grin. "Looked like you needed a barkeeper."

"Does my wife know you're here?"

McLaughlin drained the shot in one gulp and set the glass down. "Haven't seen her. Just got here a few minutes ago. The door was open, but nobody answered when I called out."

"Leave the money on the bar when you're finished." Patrick rushed for the stairs. She had to be in bed, asleep. She wasn't on that train.

Her door stood ajar. He slammed it open. It struck the wall with a loud bang that reverberated through the building. "Charm?"

No petticoats piled on the unmade bed. No suitcases. The floors, he could see them. Nothing of hers remained.

His heart jerked in panic. He whirled around, didn't

bother to look in his room. He knew she wouldn't be there. She had boarded that train, and he could guess who was with her.

LaBar.

The departure whistle sounded.

Terror such as he'd never known before surged through him. God only knew what that bastard had threatened to coerce Charm into going with him. Patrick took the stairs two at a time and headed out the door. Blocking out the stabbing pain, he loped in the direction of the train.

Smoke billowed from the locomotive's diamond stack. A conductor at the bottom of the steps leading up to the parlor car stopped him. "You have a ticket?"

Patrick fisted his hands. He restrained a mad urge to knock the obstruction out of his way. "I don't need a ticket. My wife is in there. I'm taking her off the train."

The conductor regarded him with a dubious frown, but then he moved to one side. "All right, but hurry…we're leaving soon as Mr. Hardt boards."

Patrick climbed the steps. His hip screamed in protest and his right leg felt like it was on fire. He entered the parlor car, panting from the pain. The interior smelled like oiled wood. Paneled walls, cushioned benched. LaBar traveled in styled.

In the rear, the seats faced each other. Patrick spotted the bearded man in the expensive suit at the same time the man saw him. Had to be LaBar. Couldn't see who sat opposite, but Charm was so short she could be concealed behind the high-backed bench.

The man slipped his hand inside his coat.

Patrick cursed his negligence. He should've thought to retrieve his gun before he left. Keeping his hands at his sides to make it clear he was unarmed, he walked purposely to the rear of the car, betting LaBar wouldn't shoot him and face hanging for murder.

When he reached the seats, he looked down into Charm's chalk-white face.

"Where are you going?" he asked softly. None of this was her fault. Of that he was certain. All she had to do was trust him. Tell him she'd been threatened. He would have LaBar jailed for abducting her—after he rearranged the other man's face.

"I-I'm leaving...you-you shouldn't have come after me," she stammered, her voice barely above a whisper.

Patrick's face grew hot. "Tell me why. Did he threaten you?"

Her abductor didn't look like much of a threat. Come to think of it, ferrets didn't look dangerous either, but they had sharp teeth. Keeping that in mind would be wise.

LaBar's hand remained inside his coat. "Miss DuCharme has agreed to return with me and honor her contract. I suggest you let her."

Patrick balled his fists. He'd tear LaBar's head off if he as much as moved his arm. "Is that a threat?"

Charm tugged the bottom of his coat. "Patrick, please... Don't cause a scene. Mr. LaBar is correct. I agreed to return to fulfill the terms of my contract. There's nothing you can do."

"You're wrong about that, *wife*." He had no wish to frighten her, but he wasn't putting up with these shenanigans. Holding her eyes, he gentled his voice. "Trust me. Tell me the real reason you're leaving..."

She looked away, clasping her hands in her lap. "That is the real reason."

By God, he would throw her over his shoulder and haul her off this train...

"Let me handle it, Juliette." LaBar reached over and patted her knee.

Patrick's anger blazed. "Touch her again, and I'll break your fingers!"

Charm cringed.

His conscience flayed him for frightening her…until he realized she wasn't cringing from him. She shrank away from LaBar's touch.

A red haze descended. Patrick grabbed the filthy coward by his lapels and dragged him out of the seat. LaBar wasn't a short man, but he was slender. No match, even with two good legs.

Patrick braced his feet. He hauled back his arm, but before he could land a punch, LaBar pulled a pocket pistol. Charm screamed at the same time Patrick raised his arm to knock the shooter's aim away from her.

The gun fired near his head with an earsplitting bang.

They fought for control of the gun. Patrick slammed LaBar's hand against the back of the bench. Gripping the man's arm, he pressed his thumb against a soft spot on the wrist, applying enough pressure to make LaBar's fingers go numb.

The gun fell to the carpeted floor.

Patrick scooped it up, his ears still ringing from the blast. A peashooter, useless for the most part, but deadly at close range. Gamblers used them, and slimy night crawlers.

LaBar took a half step back, lost his balance and plopped onto the seat. "Shoot me, and you'll hang," he screeched.

It was awfully tempting.

Patrick glanced at two other men in the car, both of whom had seen the altercation. Witnesses to murder, if he did what he itched to do.

The men jumped up and left the railcar in a hurry.

"You see? They're going after the sheriff."

Charm came to her feet. She grabbed Patrick's arm, her features stark with fear. "Don't do this. It's not worth it. He's not worth your life."

Patrick tucked the gun beneath his coat into the

waistband of his trousers. He slipped his arm around his wife's waist and drew her next to him. Regret crept in on the heels of anger. He should've held his temper in check until he'd talked Charm into leaving with him. If soldiers showed up to arrest him, would Charm defend him? Or would she side with LaBar? He wasn't so sure anymore. That didn't mean he would give her up. No matter what power LaBar had over her, she couldn't leave. If she did, he knew without a doubt he would never see her again.

"No, he's not worth my life. But you are."

Chapter Ten

Charm dropped the hold she had on Patrick's vest. Her hands quivered from the shock of hearing that gun go off, thinking he'd been killed, and then fearing he'd put a bullet between Simon's eyes and she would have to watch her beloved swing by his neck at the end of a rope. He'd give her heart failure if he didn't cease being heroic.

He couldn't save her. Not without sacrificing himself.

"Get out of here!" She pushed him.

He didn't budge, immovable as a boulder.

"Let him stay," Simon taunted. "When the authorities arrive, we can tell them he attacked me."

"You pulled a gun on him, you idiot!" Regardless, she knew Simon was right. There were two witnesses who could say Patrick had started the altercation. If her husband left now and the train pulled away, he could avoid being arrested.

She turned to him, begging. "Please, go."

He tightened his hold around her waist. "I'll leave if you come with me."

"Patrick, I've already told you, I'm going back to

Chicago. You met with Mr. Hardt. He knows you're married. You don't need me anymore."

Her husband's jaw firmed. "You're wrong about that. I do need you...and not just to prove my claim."

"This is all very touching, but she's told you repeatedly to leave—"

Charm twisted, glaring at her tormenter. "Shut up Simon! You've already caused enough trouble."

Simon folded his arms, looking belligerent. "Not nearly as much as I'm going to cause."

Fear ricocheted inside her chest. She had to get Patrick out of harm's way. She was doing the right thing. "If I finish out this contract, he'll have nothing more to hold over my head. I'll be free."

Her husband's expression remained resolute. "You can be free now. There's no reason to go back."

Her heart shrank into a painful knot. Patrick had given her no choice but to be cruel. In hurting him she would wound herself, and the torment would be endless. The words stuck in her throat. Patrick had lived with pain for so long, he'd learned to endure it. She would, too. This was a part she had to play for his sake, not hers.

She gazed at him through a sneering mask. "Will you shackle me, then, and drag me off the train? Or will you let me go, like you promised."

Pain flared in his eyes...and exploded in her heart. He removed his arm from around her waist.

Burning with shame, she sat down. She couldn't bear the hurt shining in his eyes, so she stared at Simon and let him see her hatred. That was all he would ever get from her.

Patrick placed his fingers on her shoulder, a light touch, yet it made her flinch "If freedom is what you want, I won't force you to stay with me. But I'm not letting you leave with this snake."

Simon reached inside his coat.

Patrick went for the gun.

Before Charm could scream *stop*, Simon was waving a piece a paper. "This is an order from a judge that requires your wife to return with me to work out her contract. If she doesn't, she will be required to pay the sum of five thousand dollars."

Charm ventured a furtive look through her lashes to gauge her husband's reaction. Patrick's stunned expression told her what she already knew. Might as well be a million dollars. He couldn't come up with that much money. Not without selling everything he owned.

"Now you see why you must allow me to return."

"I'll pay it," Patrick shot back.

"The full amount, payable immediately." Simon's eyes gleamed with anticipation. He was enjoying Patrick's ruination.

Worse, the sacrifice wouldn't change anything. Simon would find some new way to torment her, and as long as Patrick stood in the way, her husband would never have any peace.

She unleashed her frustration on him. "I don't want you to come to my rescue, and I don't want your money. Can't you get that through your thick head?"

Patrick blinked, stunned. Her barrage had caught him by surprise.

He would leave now. Dear God, he had to leave before the soldiers showed up.

He put his hand on the arm of the bench and knelt, his movements so slow and awkward it hurt to watch. Reaching across her lap, he grasped her hand as a drowning man might clutch a rope. "You're my wife," he said roughly. "I would do anything…pay any amount…go anywhere to be with you. I love you, Charm. I should've told you that before. If I had, maybe you would trust me."

144

Her heart shrank into a painful knot. Oh God. She couldn't keep up the pretense of not caring, couldn't act like he didn't matter. He mattered more than anything in the world.

"You can't afford to pay my debt, Patrick. You'll lose the saloon. Lose everything…" Her voice cracked. "I can't let you do that and live with myself."

He twined his fingers through hers. A loose grip, but one that was stronger than the thickest rope. "I'm willing to lose everything. Except you."

Love rose as fast as floodwaters. Nothing could hold it back. Not self-doubt. Not fear. Not even regret. She tenderly stroked his hair. "I'd give up everything for you, Patrick. Don't you see? That's why I left."

Simon shifted forward, his nostrils flaring, as if he smelled his prey escaping. "You have to come back, or I can have you jailed." He started to reach out. Perhaps he intended to take hold of her skirt or her hand, or maybe wring her neck.

Patrick came over the bench with an animalistic growl. He grabbed Simon's forefinger and gave it a violent twist.

Simon's shriek echoed off the wood-paneled walls. He jerked his hand from Patrick's grip and hugged it to his chest. "You sonofabitch! You broke my finger!"

The veins on Patrick's neck bulged as he hovered over Simon with his hands fisted. "I'll break your *neck* the next time you dare to touch my wife."

Simon's face turned ashen, sweat sheened his forehead. Now he knew what pain felt like. "By God, you'll pay for this! I'll see to it that you both rot in jail."

"What's the problem here?" The deep voice came from behind.

Mr. Hardt. Someone had sent for the railroad agent, or he heard the gunshot when he boarded. Maybe that's why the train hadn't left the station. He rested his hand on the back of the bench, looking down at her quizzically. "Mrs. O'Shea? Can I be of assistance?"

"That oaf broke my finger," Simon shouted. "And he tried to kill me."

"After you provoked him and shot at him." Charm pinned a hard look on the sweaty, pale-faced bully sitting across from her. He could threaten her, try to intimidate her, sue her or even see her put in jail. But he could no longer hurt her, because he couldn't touch her heart.

Old fears fell away, the chains broken. Love hadn't bound her…it had set her free.

Patrick rested his hand on her shoulder. Without saying anything, he let her know he was there, and would always be there.

"This is Mr. LaBar," she said to the railroad agent. "He came to town to tell me that if I didn't return and fulfill my contract, he would have me jailed and sue my husband for the money I owe him. But I don't owe him anything. He stole my inheritance, and then he made sure I never saw a cent of my earnings. He's a bully and a cheat."

"I have a judge's order," Simon shot back. He hunched over his hand, tucked protectively against him like a broken wing.

Mr. Hardt's face remained expressionless. "May I see this order?" He extended his hand.

Simon hesitated. "Who are you?"

"Ross Hardt, land agent for the Gulf Railroad."

Simon fumbled inside his coat and produced the paper. He leveled a murderous look at Charm as he handed it over.

Hardt perused the document. "Judge Kirkpatrick… Yes, I've heard of him. He's a state judge in Illinois. He has no jurisdiction in Kansas."

"How would you know?" Simon snapped.

"My business is to know the law."

A flicker of hope reignited. Mr. Hardt's knowledge appeared to be superior to Simon's. Even more surprising, he seemed inclined to believe her.

Patrick motioned for Charm to move over and sat down. He draped his arm around her shoulders and leaned close. "Just so you know, I'm not giving you up. If it comes to a fight we'll do battle together." His brows gathered in a fierce frown. "*Faugh-a-bellagh!*"

Clear the way! She recalled every detail of his story about the terrible battle. He had taken on enemies against impossible odds and survived; wounded and scarred, yet somehow stronger.

She put her hand on his chest, over his heart. "You never give up, do you?"

"Never." He gave her a dark smile. "I've gone through hell once. If necessary, I'll do it again."

"That won't be necessary, Mr. O'Shea." The railroad agent folded the order. "Mr. LaBar has no authority to remove your wife from the state. He's welcome to pursue the matter through legal channels. In the meantime, I'll ask my friend, Alan Pinkerton, to make inquiries about this order, and about his financial arrangements with a judge who is under investigation for taking bribes."

Simon made an inarticulate sound. His face turned very red.

Charm gaped at the agent, flabbergasted, and then, overjoyed. If there was proof that Simon had bribed a judge, why, he would be the one put in jail. Not her.

Mr. Hardt tucked the order into his pocket and continued to address Simon. "I suggest you go back to wherever you came from, and if you value your freedom, never return."

Unsmiling, the railroad agent addressed her. "Would you and Mr. O'Shea care to join me in my private car?

Charm couldn't move fast enough.

Hardt's private railcar looked nothing like the coach car she'd arrived in, or the parlor car where she'd been with Simon. Rather, half the car had been turned into an office, complete with table, chairs and a desk strewn with papers and maps. Behind a wall, she assumed he had a sleeping berth or other living space. Nothing indicated he was anything other than what he seemed—all work and no nonsense.

His defense touched Charm deeply. She understood the reason he might've come to check on the situation, but she couldn't fathom why he would help them. She hadn't thought he had much compassion. Considering she'd been wrong about Patrick, maybe her first impression of Mr. Hardt had been wrong, too. "Thank you, sir…for everything."

"My pleasure, Mrs. O'Shea." Hardt crossed to a liquor cabinet near the desk and uncorked a crystal decanter. He poured what looked like brandy into two glasses and handed one to Patrick. "Here's to two problems solved."

"Two problems?" Patrick took the glass.

"Come by the office day after tomorrow. I'll have your claim, signed by the directors."

Patrick whooped.

Charm's heart grew lighter. Thank God, her husband's land would be secured. One less worry. "The other problem, you mean Simon." She was relieved to be away from him, but knew better than to turn her back. "I'm afraid he won't give up. He'll be back with reinforcements."

Hardt appeared unconcerned. "I wouldn't worry about Simon LaBar. When I reach Fort Scott, I'll send off a telegraph to Pinkerton. They'll keep him busy enough that he won't have time to bother you."

Patrick clinked his glass against Hardt's. "May those

who love us love us, and those that don't love us may God turn their hearts; and if He doesn't turn their hearts, may he turn their ankles, so we'll know them by their limping."

"Or by their bent fingers," Charm suggested. "If I may, I'd like to join you in a toast…"

Mr. Hardt arched his eyebrows. Then he handed his glass to her without a word. He hadn't offered her a drink, probably because ladies weren't expected to want one. Nor were they encouraged to become actresses and lead independent lives. Her husband hadn't tried to make her into the perfect Victorian woman. He loved her for who she was, and was willing to do anything to prove his love—and she felt the same way about him.

She raised her glass. "Here's to my husband, who never gives up."

The drink burned all the way down. She couldn't speak. For a moment, she couldn't breathe.

Patrick rubbed her back. "Are you all right?"

"What is that stuff?" She gasped, still trying to catch her breath.

"Whiskey," the railroad agent answered. "My special collection."

Grimacing, she handed him the glass. "I thought it was brandy."

"Let me get you some." He returned to the liquor cabinet.

His *special* whiskey had burned a hole in her throat. She wasn't taking a chance on his brandy. Charm lifted her hand in surrender. "No, thank you."

"Water?"

"That would be fine."

Patrick took the water glass and handed it to her. "Mr. Hardt, you're a decent man. I thank you for what you did. We won't ever forget your kindness."

"Don't be too quick to credit me with kindness,"

Hardt replied evenly. "I never do anything without expecting to be repaid."

Patrick didn't look offended by the crass comment. He smiled like he found the remark amusing. "So what do I owe you?"

The agent tossed back his whiskey. He didn't blink. "Stay in Centralia. Open that theater I've been hearing about...and don't host any more Land League meetings."

Chapter Eleven

Patrick awoke Sunday morning with his wife in his arms. He heaved a sigh of utter contentment, could think of nothing better than waking with Charm curled up next to him. Well, there might be one thing better.

He shifted his arm to bring her closer and kissed the top of her head.

"Mmmm," she murmured.

"Are you awake?" he asked, hopeful.

She stretched her arm across his chest, nuzzling his shoulder. The soft touch of her lips sent prickles skittering across his bare skin. "If I say no, will you let me sleep? I promise, I'll be more energetic later."

Smiling, he twirled a finger in her hair. "As energetic as you were last night?"

She rose up on her arms and regarded him sleepy-eyed. "Are you always this chipper in the morning?"

"Are you always a sleepyhead?"

With a groan, she put her face down, forehead on her arms. He ran his hand over her hair, stroking. "Poor *stóirín*," he murmured. "We'll have to find a compromise."

"Noon," came the muffled answer.

Patrick chuckled. He would never be able to lay abed for that long. His back and leg would get too stiff. Right now, though, his attention was on another part that was getting stiff. But his wee darling needed her sleep, so he would compromise.

She rested her head on his chest and stretched out her arm, reaching around his side to hold him. "I can hear your heart beating," she said softly.

"It's saying *I love you*. And it will for as long as it beats."

"Then I hope it beats forever, because that's how long I'm going to love you."

His heart pounded harder. He'd thought luck had failed him, that God had turned His back. Then Charm dropped into his life. He would never doubt goodness again.

"I've been thinking about what you said, about wanting to travel and perform. I can settle with McGill on a price for the saloon. We can travel wherever you want, get you performances in big theaters. I'll help you. Be your manager, your assistant, whatever you want to call it."

She blinked at him, incredulous. Now she was wide-awake. "Why would you do that?"

"If it's what's you want, then it's what I want. That's how love works." He smiled at her astonished expression. "You might even decide you like mornings."

She didn't laugh at his joke. "You can't sell this place to a dishonest man. No more than I can go back to Simon. Besides, we promised Mr. Hardt we'd stay and open a theater."

That reason didn't sit well with him. He wasn't forcing his wife to bend her life around to suit the whims of a railroad agent, no matter what the man had done for them.

"Is that why you're willing to stay? Because you promised him?"

"No, I'm willing to stay because I promised you." A mischievous twinkle came into her eyes. "And because you'll promise to turn the saloon into a grand theater and name it after me."

An insistent knocking got them out of bed.

"I'm going to kill whoever that is. They should know better than to bother newlyweds this early in the morning..." Charm grumbled as she dressed hurriedly. She and Patrick had just taken up where they'd left off last night when someone started hammering on the door.

Patrick had dressed and gone to answer. It was probably that parasite, McLaughlin, looking for another handout. He seemed to think O'Shea's was his second home.

She dragged a brush through her hair and twisted it up, jabbing hairpins into the bun. Patrick would be nice because he couldn't be any other way. She, however, would send their unwanted guests to perdition with a tongue-lashing. Then she and her husband could get back to more pleasant activities.

Still grumbling, she headed down the stairs—and halted at the back door into the saloon. A strange sight greeted her.

Patrick held the front door open as Susannah, Hope, Delilah, Prudence and Rose filed inside. They carried trays of food, along with cakes and pies.

"Where can we put these?" Susannah asked him.

Without a word, he motioned to the bar.

He'd reported seeing Susannah and Prudence several days ago, and said they had been told a different story about why she left the hotel. She hadn't expected them to actually come to the saloon. Prudence spotted her first, and started over with a very determined look on her face.

Growing nervous, Charm reached up to straighten the bun. She smoothed her hands over the light cotton dress she'd thrown on, the first thing she could find.

The other woman had dressed in their Sunday finery. Maybe that's what this was, a Sunday school meeting. After all, Patrick had agreed to let the preacher use the saloon on Sundays.

Prudence wrung her hands, appearing uncertain. "Hello Charm… I owe you an apology for believing you would leave without saying goodbye, and for not coming by to check on you. Will you forgive me?"

The reason for their sudden appearance sank in. They were here to see her, and to extend an olive branch. The doubt and hurt coating Charm's heart melted away.

"How could I not?" She opened her arms and her friend stepped into them.

"Oh, I'm so happy to see you, and I'm glad you're not angry." Prudence stepped back with tears running down her cheeks. She fished a handkerchief from beneath her sleeve and wiped her eyes. "We were told you left, and that you didn't want to see us anymore. I should've known better."

"Yes, you should have…" Charm started solemnly, then smiled with affection. "But I forgive you. If you forgive me."

"For what?"

"For not having faith in our friendship."

The other women approached and made their apologies.

"We missed your wedding. So we've come to surprise you with a reception." Susannah hugged her. "We are still friends, aren't we?" she whispered.

Tears filled Charm's eyes. Her friends demonstrated courage and humility in coming here to ask for forgiveness. She had as much need of forgiveness, and for their friendship. "Yes, we will always be friends."

"We've brought you gifts, too." Hope gestured to a table where several boxes were stacked.

"Things you might be able to use to set up your home," Delilah added.

Their thoughtfulness and generosity left Charm speechless.

Patrick gave her an *I-told-you-so* grin before he started taking chairs off tables. "You ladies can sit here.

Rose appeared beside Charm. She leaned down, whispering. "Remember, dear sister, The Order of the Garter. We stand by each other, always. Now you have to give the garter to the next woman who marries. Who do you think it will be? Delilah? Hope? Susannah?"

Charm's gaze found the leader of the group, who had rounded up the others to move the food to the table. As usual, she was giving orders. She wouldn't be an easy catch. It would take a man equally hardheaded. None she would accept came to mind. "No, I think…"

Prudence set out two pies, which she probably baked. That woman could cook.

"Maybe Prudence? If we can get her out of the kitchen long enough to meet a suitable man."

"Any ideas?"

The only man who came to mind was the flirtatious rascal who had set off Patrick's temper. But no, that wouldn't be a good match. Mr. Childers had a wild reputation, not to mention being a bootlegger. Prudence wouldn't know what to do with a man like that.

"Let me think on it."

Patrick stepped onto the stage. "Attention everyone! I have an announcement to make." He motioned for Charm to join him, and then draped an arm around her shoulders, his embrace forming an affectionate, protective shelter.

She slipped her arm around his waist, offering him the same.

"We plan to turn O'Shea's into a theater," he announced. "We'll have shows and plays, and make it place women can attend."

The ladies clapped loudly.

"Our theater needs a name, and my wife suggested one earlier today…"

Charm turned to look at him, and he winked at her. Oh heavens, he hadn't taken her seriously, had he?

"Welcome, everyone, to *O'Shea's Good Luck Charm*."

Look for future books in

The Bride Train Series

VALENTINE'S ROSE

PATRICK'S CHARM

Coming this summer, book 3:
TEMPTING PRUDENCE

Find out more about the series at my website
www.eeburke.com

Also by E.E. Burke

American Mail-Order Brides Series

VICTORIA, BRIDE OF KANSAS

SANTA'S MAIL-ORDER BRIDE

Steam! Romance and Rails Series

PASSION'S PRIZE
(with Jennifer Jakes and Jacqui Nelson)

KATE'S OUTLAW
(a novella included in Passion's Prize)

HER BODYGUARD

A DANGEROUS PASSION

FUGITIVE HEARTS

www.eeburke.com

To learn about upcoming and new releases, please join
my newsletter:
https://www.eeburke.com/news.html

E.E. Burke is an award-winning author of sexy and heartwarming historical romance featuring emotionally complex characters in settings rich with historical detail. Her latest series of sweet romances, *The Bride Train*, features a cast of unusual characters thrown together through a misguided bride lottery. *Steam! Romance and Rails* is a sexy series that follows the lives of dangerous men and daring women caught up in a cutthroat railroad competition. Think "Hell On Wheels" with happier endings.

Her novella, Victoria, Bride of Kansas, is part of the unprecedented American Mail-Order Brides Series penned by forty-five top Western romance authors. Victoria, Bride of Kansas reached #1 in Victorian and Western Romance and #4 in Historical Romance on Amazon's top sellers lists.

E.E., also known as Elisabeth, has earned accolades in regional and national contests, including the RWA's prestigious Golden Heart®. Over the years, she's been a disc jockey, a journalist and an advertising executive, before finally getting around to living the dream—writing stories readers can get lost in.